SARA'S SLEEP

my publi... novella!

Terri Sonoda

TERRI SONODA

adoro books

www.adorobooks.com

Published by
ADORO BOOKS
June/2012

Adoro Books
Moncks Corner, SC
www.adorobooks.com

Copyright © 2012 by Theresa Sonoda

Published in the United States by Adoro Books
An imprint of Escrit Lit, LLC

ISBN 978-0984800322

*The book is dedicated to my Dad. He is,
and always has been, my hero and my rock.*

Chapter One

Sara awoke to the aroma of fresh coffee. She had to think for a second, and then remembered Mark, her husband, was finally home. She quickly swung herself out of bed, donned her robe and found her slippers. Her legs felt as if they were tied with weights. She needed to have a long, overdue talk with Mark. Things hadn't been right between the two of them for some time and Sara had been planning on how to approach the subject.

She hurried through her bathroom morning ritual, leaving the make-up and hair-styling for later. Everything felt like it was moving in slow motion. It seemed like forever before she reached the kitchen. "Baby, I'm glad you're home. I need to talk to you about something and it cannot wait," she said. She heard the car start just outside and realized her husband wasn't there. Her well-meaning neighbor had stopped in and put on the coffee before leaving for work.

Mark was not there. He would never be there again. Her head reeling from her apparent hallucination and her body void of any energy, Sara slumped into the chair at the kitchen table. Her mind was flooded by thoughts of the previous few days. Mark had been killed in a car accident on Tuesday, the funeral had been on Friday, and here it was Sunday, and Sara didn't know anything. She didn't know what to do next, and she surely didn't want to do anything but just go back to bed. Everyone had been stopping by with their condolences and all she wanted to do was lock herself away from it all, from the world and all those sad faces.

Every night, she had tried to find solace in sleep, but sleep would not come. The previous night, she had drunk a whole bottle of Chardonnay and a shot of whiskey, followed by a sleeping pill, and still awoke every few minutes during the night. Once she found deep sleep, the nightmares came, so she never really had any rest, except for the short naps she took resting her head on the kitchen table throughout the day. She ate very little and what she did eat often came back up. The depression and lack of rest added years to her face and she no longer seemed to care much about her personal hygiene or grooming. Her grief was affecting her physically and it showed.

She just wanted her thoughts to go away. Why was her body so tired and yet her mind in overdrive?

She thought back to the previous week, when Mark had left for his meeting upstate. They had argued and she remembered thinking, "Good riddance," as his car left the driveway. That was her last memory of him. How could that be her very last memory? She hadn't even tried calling him while he was away. Their lives had become so inconsequential, so disconnected. When Mark had first begun his sales career, they had talked on the phone several times every day that he was away on business. Now they rarely talked unless there was something that needed attention. This last business trip there was no phone call—only the appearance of two police officers at her door. Their words would be ingrained in her memory forever.

"Morning ma'am. Are you Sara Billings?"

"Yes. What can I do for you?"

"I'm Officer Browne and this is Officer Stevenson. We regret to inform you that your husband has been killed in an accident. We are so very sorry, ma'am. Is there anyone we can call for you?"

Chapter Two

"Come down from there this minute, Jenny! Right now! I mean it. You come down or else!" Sara yelled at the girl perched on a limb way too high up in the tree. She looked on in horror as the young girl inched her way farther out on the limb, trying to retrieve her beloved pet cat, Snickers.

"Mommy, I have to get Snickers. She's scared and she won't come down," replied the girl, with no fear in her voice. Closer and closer she inched to the end of the branch where the cat was perched.

Sara could see the cat's furry tail swaying underneath the branch. The limb was far too thin and surely would not hold the weight of the cat and the child. Shaking, Sara continued pleading with the girl. "Honey, Snickers has climbing powers we don't have. She will find her way down safely. Now please don't move anymore. Just stay where you are."

A loud crackle pierced the air and Sara could see Jenny grab the branch and hold on tight, fear now showing in her big blue eyes.

"Mommy! I'm scared! Mommy, get me down. Please Mommy. Get me down!"

Jenny clung to the branch while Sara dialed 911. The number kept ringing and ringing with no answer. She tried the number again. Ringing. No answer. Why was no one answering 911?

The cat let out a screech as the branch broke. Jenny screamed, "Mommy! Mommy!" and began to fall. Falling. Falling. Sara ran to try and catch her.

"Mom. Mom. Mom. Are you okay Mom?"

Sara awoke to her daughter shaking her. She was drenched in cold sweat and had to think for a moment to figure out where she was. Thank God it was only a dream! Her Jenny was grown and standing before her, looking quite concerned, but she was okay. There was no tree and no fall. Relief swept over Sara.

"Mom, what's wrong? We were supposed to go to breakfast together, and when you didn't pick me up, and you wouldn't answer your phone, I came over. You seemed to be having a nightmare, Mom. Are you okay? I'm worried about you," said Jenny as she helped her Mom with her slippers.

"I'm okay honey. I just had a bad dream," answered Sara, but she wanted to say, "I haven't been sleeping well and when I do sleep, I dream bad things. I don't know how to make it stop, and it's exhausting me." She didn't want to scare her daughter, so she kept quiet about the insomnia.

Her beautiful daughter was all she had left. Jenny was a strong young woman, but she had just lost her father. Sara felt that she didn't need to shoulder her mom's drama right now. Jenny had always been close with her parents and had been very protective of them. Sara gazed at her daughter's beautiful face and her heart filled with love. Jenny had been a model daughter, never giving her parents a minute of trouble.

"Mom, it's been three weeks now since Dad passed away and you haven't been out of the house. I'm worried about you. Maybe we should schedule a spa day together or maybe you might want to take up your sketching again. The days have been gorgeous with all the leaves turning. You don't want to miss the opportunity to capture the beauty of the fall colors, do you? I know how you love autumn!" Jenny knew she was babbling, but wanted to say something that might trigger her mother back to reality.

Sara sat and gazed at her daughter while she ran on about her worries. Jenny was the most wonderful and precious result of her 35-year marriage to

Mark. They hadn't been able to have any more children, so Jenny had become their center of attention, their core. A couple's core was supposed to be their love for one another, but not in Sara and Mark's case. It was most definitely their beloved Jenny. Once Jenny grew up and moved out on her own, their home and their marriage had become one of silence and distance. Still, Sara had loved Mark; she just didn't show it as she should have. Mark hadn't exactly been a doting romantic either. In fact, even when in the same room, keeping her at a distance had become routine for him … and for her.

"Mom?" asked Jenny as she looked into Sara's face. "Have you heard a word I've said? Let's finish getting you dressed and go have a late breakfast. I have some news and I want to deliver it over a nice Mimosa and a spinach omelet. How's that sound, Mom?"

Sara forced a weak smile and replied, "I'm in the mood for a double latte this morning, myself."

"Double latte it is, Mom. Now let's go!" Jenny said, leading her mom out to the car.

As they backed out of the driveway, Sara noticed the giant tree peeking over the house from the back yard and she shuddered. She was so weary from lack of sleep.

But sleep brought the dreams.

7

Chapter Three

"A baby?" asked Sara, her hand shaking as she returned the coffee cup to the table, its contents spilling over onto the festive tablecloth. "Where did this come from? Why would you want a baby now, Jenny? You have no husband and no viable prospects as far as I know. Do you? For crying out loud, why can't you start with a cat or a dog? Or a bird? I hear birds are great companions and low maintenance. But a baby? You have no idea how hard it is to take care of a baby. And by yourself, Jenny? You haven't a clue, have you?"

Jenny stared at her mother in disbelief as she went on and on. She'd never seen her mom like this before.

"Jenny, you've only just lost your father. Is this some way of filling a void in your life? I don't understand. I just don't understand." Sara took in a breath, and Jenny found her opportunity to speak.

"Mom, if you would only let me get a word in edgewise, I would explain," pleaded Jenny. Before her mom could protest, she continued, "I just want a baby, Mom. I don't want a husband. And I don't need to fill Dad's void. And a dog or cat? Seriously Mom? I'm thirty-two years old. My clock's ticking and my egg supply depletes with each day that passes. I want a baby. And I desperately want you to understand. We could do this together. This could enrich both our lives so much! And I think the sperm bank is an excellent option."

Jenny's voice seemed to fade as Sara felt the vertigo she'd been cursed with since sleeplessness had taken over her life. Both hands on the table to steady herself, she closed her eyes for a moment, hoping the dizziness would pass. She hadn't eaten and was feeling nauseated with the smell of the eggs in front of her.

Sara felt her daughter shaking her awake, for the second time that day.

"Mom, wake up. Oh my god, Mom, what's going on with you?" The look on her face revealed her concern. "You fell sound asleep sitting straight up, Mom. I am worried about you. We should be at the hospital, not here. Let's go, now!" Jenny tried to wave the waiter down and Sara took her hand.

"Honey, I'm okay. I'm just very tired. These past weeks have drained my energy and apparently, my reserve."

Jenny was watching and listening, but she wasn't buying Sara's story. "Mom, you sleep at the table. You miss appointments. You don't even talk and reason with me the way you used to. And you go off on these rants. I've never seen you like this and quite frankly, it's scaring the hell out of me. Please, please, let me take you to the doctor."

Jenny wasn't backing down. Sara didn't understand why she even wanted her to. She did need help, after all. She just didn't want Jenny fretting over her. And now, this business of her wanting a baby? It was all Sara could do to remain cognizant at this point, so she relented.

"All right. I will make an appointment and you can go with me. I promise. Today, however, I just want to go home. Is that okay? Turns out, I'm just not hungry. And we'll talk about the baby later, don't you worry about that. I have plenty more to say on that subject, young lady!" Sara said, trying to lighten the tone of the conversation. She really could handle this herself. She would go to the doctor. Just not yet. She just wanted to go home.

"Sure Mom, I'll take you home, but I will be accompanying you to the doctor soon." The crisis seemingly averted, Jenny offered, "Want to cut through the park on the way home so we can enjoy the fall colors? I haven't driven through there lately, but I hear the colors are especially bright this year. Lots of fiery oranges and reds."

"That sounds lovely, dear. Let's drive through the park." Sara smiled. She loved her Jenny so very much. Jenny was all she had left. Her recent nightmares had all been of Jenny being in harm's way. Each time, she woke up just before the looming presence culminated in some unknown horrific ending. She always woke up in an icy-cold sweat, disoriented, frightened and alone. Every night, it took her longer and longer to fall asleep, resulting in her inability to assess time or adapt to any of her normal routine. She had always been a woman of routine, one who always accomplished things in a timely manner and with impeccable results. Her life now was, indeed, no longer her own.

"Aren't the trees beautiful, Mom! Look at those over there! Amazing!" Jenny pointed toward the trees on her right and looked over for her mom's approval. "Mom, are you asleep again? Mom?" Her mother appeared sound asleep. She reached over to touch her cheek and found her face hot to the touch.

Sara's breathing was shallow and sweat was streaming down alongside her face and onto her neck. She began to mumble, her head bobbing down on her chest as if it were weighted down. Drool was seeping out one side of her mouth. Jenny stepped on the gas, headed out of the park and straight toward the hospital. She was getting to the bottom of this, with or without her mom's approval.

"No Jenny! Not the baby! Give me the baby, Jenny! Just hand me the baby! No, No! Jenny, no!" screamed Sara as they wheeled her into the emergency room on a gurney. Sara appeared to be awake but was lost deeply inside her nightmare.

Jenny was standing on a ledge, several stories off the ground, holding her baby, and swearing she'd throw her baby off the building if Sara came any closer. "You don't love me anymore, Mom. You just love the baby. The baby! I'm so sick of this baby. It cries all the time. And you want my baby, don't you, Mother? You don't want me anymore, do you? The baby has taken my place. You dream about the baby now, don't you? You don't dream about me anymore. Well, you can't have my baby. No one can have him. He belongs to me, and I don't belong to anyone!" And with that, Jenny calmly turned and jumped.

"She's stopped breathing!" shouted the paramedic. With medical personnel and equipment crowded around her mother, Jenny stared on in horror, through her own stream of tears. What in the hell was going on?

Chapter Four

"Good morning, sleepyhead!" remarked Jenny, smiling at her mother who had just opened her eyes.

"Hi, honey," Sara mumbled weakly as she looked around the room. "What's wrong? What happened?" Sara attempted to sit up in bed. Dizziness took over, however, and she slumped back onto her pillow. At this point, Sara knew one thing—she was in a hospital. She tried to recollect how she might have ended up there, but thoughts were not coming easily. After a couple more feeble attempts at sitting upright, she finally succumbed to the apparent reality of the situation, and settled for assessing her surroundings.

"Mom, you are here because exhaustion, lack of sleep, and dehydration caused your body to give out. You also had a severe blood pressure hike and seizures. You caused quite a scare in the ER when you stopped breathing for a few seconds," Jenny said softly, stroking her Mom's hair. It was hard for her to choke back the tears, but she managed. Her mom had enough to worry about without watching her lose it. She'd almost lost her mother! She still couldn't wrap her head around the last few days.

Sara stared at her daughter in disbelief. "I did what?"

"Yes Mom," Jenny continued, "your insomnia apparently was a much bigger issue than you'd let on. They are still running tests but I'm willing to bet you'll be getting your ass chewed by the doctor really soon." She smiled at Sara, so relieved she was okay. She was okay, wasn't she? Jenny couldn't shake a feeling she'd had since her mom awoke. Something was just not right. "And furthermore, I am pretty sure you haven't been eating enough. You're skin and bones. So tell me, are you trying to send me to an early grave? You've already scared the shit out of me. What's next?"

Sara's comprehension was a bit foggy, but she strained to remain focused and hopefully get some answers. "I'm sorry, honey. I just wasn't able to sleep no matter what I tried. It made me sick, so of course I wasn't hungry. The more tired I became, the more skewed my thought processes were. I remember sitting at the kitchen table a lot, but to tell you the truth, my memory of it all is pretty vague." She was trying to connect with her daughter, but she had no intention of telling her about her nightmares, even now. Maybe she was over the bad dreams. "How long have I been here, Jenny?" She was almost afraid to ask, but had to know.

"Three days! The longest three days of my life, I might add!" said Jenny with a forced smile. She was trying to lighten things a bit. After all, she had just laid a lot of scary information on her mom.

"Well, I do feel rested, somewhat. I'd just about forgotten that feeling—being rested. I like it," said Sara, following her daughter's lead with a little levity. She really did feel better than she had in a very long time. Was it medication? Did they have her all doped up? Well, whatever they were giving her, she wanted to take home a gallon of it.

"Good morning ladies!" interrupted Dr. Martin, sporting a brilliant smile and a charming bedside manner that did not go unnoticed. "I heard our Sleeping Beauty has awakened and I had to pop in for the celebration. Welcome back Mrs. Billings! How are you feeling?"

"Hi, Doctor. I'm feeling a bit groggy but otherwise, fine. In fact, I'm starving. That's a good sign, right?" Sara asked. She thought he might very well be one of the best looking doctors she'd ever seen. He'd give McDreamy on *Grey's Anatomy* a real run for his money, that's for sure. She guessed him to be in his early forties, and there was no wedding ring. The Cupid in her was already conjuring up a match-making plan for Jenny and the Doc.

Sara looked over at her daughter, expecting her to look as impressed with Dr. Martin as she was.

The last thing on Jenny's mind was romantic prospects. "Doctor, have all the tests come back? Do you know anything further about Mom's condition? When can I take her home? I'll be staying with her so just let me know anything I need to be doing for her."

Sara cut in, "Well that's news to me, Jenny. You don't need to turn your life upside-down for me. I'm going to be fine."

Dr. Martin wasn't getting a word in. He just looked back and forth between the two women, seemingly engrossed in their conversation.

"Sorry, Mom. Done deal. I'm staying with you for a while. Besides, I could use a little quality mom/daughter time. It'll be like a mini vacay for us girls, only at home. We'll have fun. I totally miss your cooking," said Jenny. She knew from the look on her mom's face she had won this battle.

Sara looked at Dr Martin. "Looks like I'll be well looked-after, Doctor. Can I go home soon?"

"The tests all came back normal. You do have high-blood pressure and will need to remain on blood pressure medication to keep that under control. I want you to continue to rest and get plenty of sleep. I'm prescribing something to help you fall asleep. Take it as needed, and please drink plenty of water. Be mindful of that because you were dehydrated when you came in and that exacerbated all your other symptoms. It's nothing to take lightly. Everything else looks okay, so I see no reason why you can't go home today. I'll get the paperwork started. Please come in to my office in a couple of weeks for follow-up, sooner if you feel the need. And, Mrs. Billings? I would also recommend your meeting with a therapist. You've been through a lot and talking with a professional could make things easier for you. I have written up a referral for you. Do you have any questions?"

Sara squelched the impulse to tell him to mind his own damned business but kept quiet. She wanted to go home … today.

Smiling, she realized she hadn't heard a fraction of what the doctor said, Sara answered, "No. I think we will manage. Thank you Doctor."

Dr. Martin squeezed Sara's hand, flashed an award-winning smile, and left.

"I'm going to see what's happened to your breakfast, Mom. Be right back," Jenny said as she also left the room.

Sara lay there, finally alone with her thoughts, making a mental list of things that needed her attention once she got home. After a few moments, she felt her eyelids grow heavy as she started drifting off to sleep. She tried to fight it as the feeling of dread slipped into her mind. "No!" she argued to herself, "No more bad dreams! Please, no more." She managed to ward off sleep, but the feeling of darkness and doom lingered. Was she going home to nightmares again? Would she do this damage to herself all over again? How could she stop this hell? Sweating, her pulse racing, she met the concerned gaze of her daughter as she entered with the breakfast tray.

"What's wrong Mom? Should I get the nurse?" Jenny slammed the tray down and started out the door.

"No, honey, come back. I'm okay, but I have something I need to talk to you about. Come here, sit on the bed with me. Come. Come on. Sit. Please?" begged Sara, motioning Jenny to the bed.

Nervous and curious, Jenny had a seat and quietly waited.

Her mom began: "I haven't been completely honest with you and I think it's time to come clean. The reason I can't sleep is not because of insomnia. It's dreams—horrific, graphic and heart-wrenching nightmares. With sleep comes terror so I don't sleep. I need help, Jenny."

Tears streamed down Jenny's face as she embraced her mom. "We'll get you help, Mom. I promise you that! Now tell me about these nightmares." Jenny suddenly remembered the night her mom was wheeled into the ER, yelling for Jenny to give her the baby. An icy chill ran down her spine, along with a looming fear at what she was about to hear.

Chapter Five

Sara poured herself a cup of coffee and headed to her favorite spot in the house, the kitchen table, nestled in an alcove by a charming bay window. Her husband Mark had installed the window for her some years ago, and she had enjoyed many hours in that very spot. Her thoughts went to Mark as she gazed out into the back yard. The ground was snow-covered and the only color in the yard was a weathered old yellow swing. Sara remembered how she and Mark had spent many warm summer evenings sitting in the swing together, holding hands, and talking of their hopes and dreams. God, how she missed him.

"Good morning, Mom," said Jenny. "You look like you are a million miles away. What's on your mind?"

"Good morning honey. Oh I was just thinking about that old tree. I think I'll have it cut down and replaced with some nice flowering bushes. What do you think?" Sara lied. She wasn't ready to talk about life without Mark, not yet, and certainly not with Jenny. Sara felt a guilty pang as she really had no idea how her daughter was adjusting to Mark's death. She'd been dealing with her own demons, after all, and they had been running the show.

"Why would you want to do that Mom? I love that old tree! I used to climb up to that first big branch and hang upside down, remember? That tree's part of the family, Mom!" Jenny wasn't about to let the tree go without a fight. "Besides, I dream about my little girl or boy climbing it someday."

Sara hadn't told Jenny the specifics of her nightmares, so her daughter didn't know about the ones where she fell from the tree. There had been many dreams of Jenny falling from that tree, each one a little different, and each one ending before Jenny fell to the ground. Sara shuddered. "No, the tree is massive and takes over the whole yard. The sun hardly gets through. It's hideous really. Don't you see that?"

"Mom, don't get upset. Where did that come from? I just said I like the old tree. If you want it gone, we will make it gone. I didn't realize it was that big of an issue for you," said Jenny, once again trying to soothe her mother's fears without having a clue as to their real meaning. "Flowering bushes would be nice and maybe a little pond or fountain. What do you think?"

"Yes! A little pond. And we'll have it stocked with some pretty fish. I'd like that," said Sara, trying to connect with her daughter on a softer level.

"What's on your schedule today, Mom?" asked Jenny, checking her phone. "I have a meeting at work, and then a hair appointment. I should be home before supper. When's your next appointment with Dr. Gerard? I would like to go with you."

"It's tomorrow at 10, but you don't need to go with me anymore, dear. I'm doing much better and you have much better things to do!" offered Sara.

"I want to be there for you. It's no trouble. And I know you're feeling better and making progress, but the doctor thinks you need to talk more. You never really told me much about those nightmares either. Don't you think it would be better if you talked about them?"

"Jenny, I told you the nightmares were horrific and they were about people I loved and that should be enough. I don't want to go over every detail. It would be like living through them again. That's what it was like for me, as if I was living them. I don't want to talk about them. I haven't had a nightmare since we got home, and I'm sleeping and taking my medication." Sara was getting defensive again.

It was unsettling to Jenny but she didn't want to push. "I know, Mom. You're doing very well. I just want you to know that I'm here for you," said Jenny. This conversation was not over. Oh it was for now, but it would come up again, as it had before.

"I'll go to the doctor on my own, but thanks for offering. Besides, after that, I am meeting an old friend for lunch. You'd be completely bored," said Sara.

"Okay, Mom. I can take a hint. Three's a crowd. Well, I'm off to work. Love you, Mom." Jenny kissed her mom on the forehead before she hurried out the door.

"Love you too my sweet girl! Be safe!" Sara yelled and waved. Then she turned her attention back to the old tree. "You're going down!" She grabbed the yellow pages and began looking through for a tree service. Slicing through the silence, the phone rang, and Sara jumped slightly in her chair.

"Hello?" said Sara. No one ever called on the land line. It was probably a telemarketer. Sara was prepared for battle.

"Hello, is this Ms. Billings?" The voice was male, and sounded all business.

"Yes it is. And who is this?" Sara waited for his response, mildly annoyed that her time was being wasted.

"This is Jim, Dr. Renna's nurse. The doctor would like to see you at your earliest convenience to discuss the test results. Can I schedule that appointment for you now, ma'am?"

"Actually, I'm sorry, this is Jenny's mother. She's not here right now, but I will ask her to call you." Sara's curiosity was up. Dr. Renna was an obstetrician.

"Yes ma'am, please ask her to call us. Thank you," said the voice. What was his name again? Sara's mind was in a fog.

"Uh, you're welcome. Have a nice day." Sara hung up the phone and poured herself another cup of coffee. Had Jenny gone ahead with her idea of trying to get pregnant? Was she pregnant? Sara's head was spinning, and she wouldn't see Jenny until suppertime. Should she call her and tell her about the phone call? Yes! She should tell her. Her daughter was seeing a baby doctor? She had to know what was going on.

"Hi, Mom. What's up?" asked Jenny from her cell. She was still in her car, having just arrived to work.

"Just wanted to tell you that Dr. Renna's nurse called and wants you to make an appointment at your earliest convenience to discuss test results. Hmmm. Anything you may have neglected to tell me?" Sara wasn't beating around the bush.

"Mom, I'm at work now. Can we talk about this tonight? I have a lot to tell you but I don't want to do it over the phone." Jenny had hoped to defer this conversation a few more weeks, but it looked like the secret was out.

"I don't think I can wait until tonight. One question. Are you pregnant?" Sara had to know. Patience had never been one of her strong points.

Jenny sat there in the parking lot, knowing she had to confess, but dreading the tirade that would most certainly follow. "Yes, I am pregnant. I'm about five weeks along. Please, Mom, don't be upset. I will explain everything when I get home. I just can't talk about this now. Love you, Mom. I gotta go."

Click. She was gone. Sara was left with the phone receiver in her hand and her mouth wide open. Sara wondered how this had gotten past her observant, intuitive eye. She certainly saw the clues now. Jenny hadn't had a glass of wine since she'd moved back in with Sara, and she'd always loved a glass of Merlot in the evenings. And? Jenny hadn't been drinking coffee, either. She'd said it upset her stomach. The little liar! Oh, Sara couldn't wait for suppertime. She had plenty to say to her daughter.

Sara knew she would never tell Jenny the whole story about the dream she had the night she was admitted into the hospital. The details were still vivid in her mind and right now, they lingered as she tried to dress and get ready for her day. No, damn it. This baby was not going to know the kind of horror that came from her nightmares! This baby was going to know love. A mother's love. And a grandmother's love.

Then it dawned on Sara, along with a sweet, almost peaceful feeling. She was going to be a grandmother!

Chapter Six

Sara was running through thick brush and trees. Running, breathless. Dragging herself along as if her body were tied to weights, she felt the sting of the wet tree branches as they slapped at her face. She had to catch up with him. She knew he had died. Why was he back and why was he taking her grandson? "Mark! Mark! Please stop! You'll hurt the baby! He needs to be home, not out in this cold. Mark! Please, please stop!" Gasping for breath, she kept putting one foot in front of the other. Something was terribly wrong; she could feel it at her core. Something dark and horrific was about to take place and she had to try and put a stop to it if it meant taking her last breath. "Mark! Please, Mark! Listen to me. He's Jenny's baby. Don't you think she will miss him? She's already lost you. How can you do this to her? Mark!" Scream as she might, he ignored her and kept running through the woods with the baby.

Sara could just barely make out a light up ahead. Was Mark taking the baby to that light? What was he going to do with her grandson? He had spoken only once since she found him standing over the baby's crib. "He's sick. He has to go. He's sick. He can't stay here." His voice had been cold as steel. She'd never known him to be so cold. Shivers ran down her spine as she used every drop of energy she had to keep following him. The baby was fine. What was he talking about? She had to catch up with him. She knew she could talk some sense into him if she just had the chance.

Sara stopped in her tracks and stared ahead. She could no longer see Mark and the baby. Just the light. It was blinding. Her head began to pound with immense pain. She dropped to her knees. Mark was dead. He died! What was she doing out there? And who was behind that light that was coming closer and closer to her?

"Mom, time to get up. Big day today. Come on, sleepyhead. Get up. I've got some muffins in the oven and the coffee's on," said a very pregnant Jenny as she entered Sara's room.

"Morning, honey. I'll be up in just a minute. My stomach's a bit upset. I just want to lie here a little while longer." Sara had her back turned to Jenny. She'd been lying there for hours after having been startled awake from the nightmare. She hadn't been able to go back to sleep, nor did she want to. She remembered her dream vividly as if it had actually happened to her. She could still feel the sting of the rain and those tree branches, and her legs ached from the running. She also needed to wash her face so Jenny wouldn't see she'd been crying. Jenny did not need to know the dreams were back. Not now.

"Mom, are you catching a cold? You sound completely hoarse. I'd better see if we have plenty of orange juice. Take your time, but hurry up, okay?"

Jenny and Sara were going to the obstetrician that day for a checkup. Only two and a half more months until the baby was due. To Jenny, it seemed like forever. The pregnancy had been a bumpy ride, with her dad passing away and her mom being hospitalized and now seeing a therapist. And then there was the baby. According to her doctor during the last appointment, the baby was much smaller than he should have been at twenty-eight weeks, and this weighed heavily on Jenny's mind.

Jenny felt a very slight stirring in her belly and smiled. The baby wasn't very active and she hardly ever felt him kick. Today he was kicking and it sent pangs of pleasure through his mother. "My little guy is going to be fine. He's a fighter," she thought, smiling again. She reminded herself, as she did every day, that she still hadn't settled on a name for the baby. Her mom was constantly riding her about this. Jenny wanted to name the baby after her father, but her mom adamantly rejected the idea. She valued her mom's opinion, but the ultimate decision was up to her. Her little boy needed to have a strong yet approachable name, one of which bullies would have no reason to mock. She thought her dad's name, Mark fit the bill, but her mom did not. Jenny had no idea why. She knew there were reasons, but with her mom's delicate condition these days, it wasn't the time to pry.

The waiting room was full when Sara and Jenny arrived at the doctor's office. Jenny checked in and they found a seat. "Let's stop by the mall after this, Mom, okay? I haven't bought anything for the baby in a couple of days. I'm going through withdrawal!" joked Jenny. Sara smiled and gazed at her daughter's jubilant face. Pregnancy became her and she radiated happiness. This baby was going to be so very welcomed and they both needed to fill a void in their lives.

"Ms. Billings?" called the nurse. Jenny and Sara got up and followed him into an examining room to await the doctor. After only a few minutes, the doctor knocked and entered.

"Good afternoon, ladies! How are you doing today?" Dr. Renna offered his hand and a smile. Sara's intuitive eyes couldn't help but notice a bit of hesitance in his voice. She looked over at Jenny, who hadn't seemed to notice at all.

"We're doing fine, Doctor. All three of us!" reported Jenny as she patted her tummy.

"Excellent! Excellent. Good to hear. Please, everyone have a seat," said the doctor as he pulled some information up on the computer. Sara continued to watch his face, which had become quite serious, yet calm. "Jenny, your baby is considerably underweight for this time in your pregnancy. I also see some inconsistencies in the testing. I don't want to alarm you, but I would like to order some further testing."

"What kind of testing, Doc?" asked Jenny, whose smile had waned, replaced with deep concern. Sara took Jenny's hand and reassured her.

"I'm sure everything's fine dear. Let the doctor explain," said Sara. She could feel the tension in Jenny's hand as she tightened her grip.

The doctor continued. "I want to run a series of blood tests, as well as schedule you for an amniocentesis. This procedure is usually done earlier, but you were young and we had no reason to run it earlier on."

"What are you looking for with this testing, Doctor?" asked Sara. Jenny said nothing.

"I'd be looking for several things: the development of the lungs; the health of the amniotic fluid with regards to infections, and any other inconsistencies that may be uncovered," said the doctor. "The baby is very small, but that does not necessarily mean there's anything wrong. This testing is to rule out those questions. Please try not to worry. That wouldn't be good for either of you or the baby."

Jenny suddenly found words. "Don't they do amniocentesis to check for developmental disabilities, such as Down Syndrome? I've read about these tests."

"Yes, the testing is also done to rule out a number of possibilities with development. But again, you should not be worried at this point. There is nothing pointing specifically to any such issues. We are only testing to become more knowledgeable, thus allowing us to take any preventive measures that may be needed." The doctor was thorough and used compassion with his explanation, and it worked, because Jenny seemed to relax a bit and accept the information.

Sara and Jenny left the doctor's office in silence, each deep in her own thoughts. No one spoke a word until they reached home and pulled into the driveway.

Sara said, "Sorry honey, I forgot to stop at the mall. I don't know where my head is today."

Jenny replied, "That's okay, Mom. I'm really not in the mood for the mall. I think I'm going to lie down for awhile." With that, she disappeared into the house.

Sara just sat there in the car, thinking about the doctor's words. Then the memory of the previous night flooded her thoughts and invaded all her reasoning.

"He's sick. He has to go. He's sick. He can't stay here." Sara couldn't get Mark's words out of her head. How was it that she had her first bad dream since the hospital stay, and it came just before this doctor's appointment? Was it some kind of a warning? No. No way. Even if she did believe in the paranormal, which she did not, she still refused to accept that her grandson was sick. Sara got out of the car, while silently cussing her dead husband for haunting her dreams. She needed to make an appointment with Doctor Gerard. She needed to sort out her thoughts, obviously, and Dr. Gerard knew how to facilitate this. The baby was going to be fine. And if he wasn't? Then she needed to be healthy in order to help her daughter through this.

"Hi, Sara! Long time no see. How are you?" Steve, her neighbor from a couple houses down, walked up the driveway and extended his hand.

Sara managed a smile and took his hand. "Hi, Steve! I'm doing quite well, thank you. How have things been going for you and the girls?" Steve was a widower. He had lost his wife to cancer some three years before.

"We're doing well but that big old house is feeling empty. The twins are away at college and Melissa is a senior and busy all the time. They don't need me as much as before, that's for sure," said Steve. Sara enjoyed his smile. He had a quiet, confident way about him that was quite attractive. She guessed him to be in his late forties. He exuded a healthy glow and the silver streaking through his hair only complimented his appearance. Sara admired a man who took care of himself.

"Oh I'm sure that is not true at all, Steve. Your girls will always need you." She smiled back at him. It was nice to have a bit of a distraction from the day's events. She would have invited him in for coffee, but needed to check on Jenny, so refrained, but did extend the offer for the next morning. "Well, I need to go. It's been far too long, Steve. We need to do some catching up. Come on over for coffee in the morning after your run, if you have time. I might even put together a healthy omelet for us!"

"You know, that sounds super! I will be here. Thank you! Well, until tomorrow, then." Steve squeezed her arm gently and continued on his way. Sara enjoyed the attention and was looking forward to the morning. She'd lost touch with so many of her friends the last few months.

Sara went upstairs and looked in on Jenny who was sound asleep. She pulled an extra blanket up over her shoulders and kissed her forehead. "Everything will be all right, baby," Sara whispered. "It has to be."

Chapter Seven

The trade winds tickled and teased at her skin. The scent of the salt air mixing with coconut oil was intoxicating. Sara was in paradise. She opened her eyes, looked down the beach and watched a young mother playing in the sand with her little ones. What a beautiful little family. But where was the father? Had he died like her Mark? Oh no, she didn't want to think about Mark! She was in paradise and such sad thoughts were not allowed. She focused on the little family. The youngest was just a toddler, clad in a droopy diaper, and tanned to a golden brown. "They must be locals," she thought. It would be glorious to live in such a beautiful place.

Feeling some heat on her back, she decided she'd better turn over to avoid burning. She adjusted her towel and chair, made herself comfortable, and reached over for her drink. "Hi, baby. Have a nice nap?" the man said in a deep voice, startling her just a bit. She looked over at Steve, taking in the visual pleasures of his bronzed, muscular frame. His legs were long and strong, toned from his daily runs. His chest was adorned with just enough hair to add ruggedness to his overall persona. She smiled as she noticed how sexy his feet looked in those flip-flops. Couldn't say that about many men, that's for sure. Sara's gaze lingered on Steve's handsome face as she slowly sipped her drink. Had she slept with him yet? Why couldn't she remember? She desperately wanted to remember.

"Mom!" shrieked Jenny from the open window in her room. Sara awoke to her daughter's unrelenting demands for more lemonade. Jenny had been ordered on bed-rest ever since the tests came back revealing the baby's under-developed lungs. Sara reluctantly got up from her lounge chair, went into the house and poured her daughter another glass of lemonade. The baby's due date was just two weeks away. Everyone was anxious for the baby to arrive, but no one more than Sara, who was both excited to be a grandmother and exhausted from waiting on her daughter hand-and-foot. Yes, baby Samuel could not arrive soon enough. Sara took the lemonade up to her daughter, wondering if they'd end up calling the baby Sammy. She figured she probably would. She loved the name on which Jenny had finally settled for the baby. Until last week, the little guy had remained nameless. Jenny had awakened one morning with the name Samuel on her tongue, and that was it. Baby Samuel it was!

"Here's your lemonade, honey. Sorry, you caught me napping on the patio. The weather is perfectly lovely today. I could make you comfortable on one of the loungers out there, if you'd like to enjoy the outdoors a bit? How about it?" offered Sara. Jenny hadn't wanted to leave the room for a couple weeks now. She really had become far too paranoid about the baby's health, in Sara's opinion. Samuel was now growing by leaps and bounds, and the doctor's prognosis was for a healthy baby. Jenny's doubts were unfounded as far as her mother was concerned.

"Thanks, Mom. Maybe tomorrow. Today I thought I'd catch up on some work emails while I'm feeling good. It's weird because I haven't felt this good in weeks. Why do you suppose that is?" asked Jenny.

"I don't know, honey, but I'm glad to hear it. I have heard old wives tales, however, of expectant mothers feeling extraordinarily good just before they gave birth. So, maybe this is a good sign? Just two more weeks! I cannot wait to meet my grandson! We need a man around this house!" Sara smiled at her daughter. Things really were going well for them lately.

Jenny gave her mom a sly, teasing smile. "We need a man, Mom? Oh really? Have you forgotten the handsome guy from down the street who keeps showing up for coffee? Have you forgotten Steve, Mom? He's a man and I am quite sure you have noticed. He's been around the house quite a bit lately. Hmmm."

"Okay, enough young lady!" giggled Sara. "Steve is just a friend, and you know that. Besides, he's almost ten years younger than I am. He doesn't see me like that. We have both lost our spouses and find comfort in each other's company. That is all."

"Sure Mom. Whatever you say." Jenny enjoyed ruffling her mother's feathers about Steve. She'd seen the sparkle he brought to Sara's eyes. She wasn't blind or stupid. Her mom had a new friend, and it would only be a matter of time before that friendship blossomed. She knew Sara could use some happiness in her life, so Jenny was completely on-board with such a union. Besides, Samuel could use a strong male role model, and Jenny certainly had no prospects to fill that role in the near future.

"Let's change the subject, shall we?" said Sara, with a finality in her voice. "I was dreaming when you woke me up." Jenny looked up with a startled concern on her face. "No, baby! It wasn't a bad dream! It was a lovely dream. I was laying on a beach, somewhere in paradise. It was so real, I could smell the salt air. It was wonderful. Thanks so much for disturbing my Shangri-la," Sara joked. She purposely neglected to mention Steve's role in her delicious dream.

"Wow, Mom. That's great! Sorry I awakened you! You haven't had a bad dream in some time, huh?" asked Jenny.

"No, not in a very long time, thank goodness. I think those days are behind me. In fact, I'm not planning on spending any more money on therapy at this time. Instead, I think I'll save that money for a real trip to paradise someday! That dream left me longing for sandy beaches and fruity rum drinks with tiny umbrellas." Sara laughed.

Jenny loved to see her mom so happy. She gazed at Sara's face, thinking how beautiful her mom was. Of course Steve would be interested in her. Who wouldn't? Now, if her mom would just see that. Jenny made a mental note to try and not interrupt her mom when Steve came over to visit. Lately, she'd been asking a lot from Sara, and sometimes selfishly so. She needed to be a bit more respectful. After all, she probably didn't need her mother to adjust her pillows and find the TV remote quite so often.

Suddenly, a knock came at the door. Sara recognized that knock and smiled to herself. It was Steve. She started downstairs, and stopped just long enough to check her reflection in the hall mirror. She wasn't wearing any makeup but her hair was fine. Steve had seen her without makeup so she wasn't going to fuss. She opened the door and greeted her friend, "Hey stranger! Long time no see!" she joked. Steve had been there for coffee earlier that day.

Steve produced a big, sexy grin and responded, "And you still look marvelous, after all this time! How do you do it?"

Sara laughed and motioned Steve into the house. They both headed for the kitchen as if they'd read each other's minds. Steve sat at the table while Sara poured them both some lemonade. She noticed some sweat glistening along Steve's forehead. Her thoughts shifted back to her paradise dream for a second. "What have you been up to today? I've been watching the workers install the pond in the back yard. I'm exhausted!" said Sara. She had had the giant old tree removed and was having a pond and some flowering bushes put in. It was late spring and she wanted flowers and light, and maybe even some decorative fish. "I'm creating my own special garden of retreat out there! Would you like to see?"

"Ankh," Steve said. One word. Sara was perplexed.

"Say what?" she retorted. Was he being a smartass? He was good at that sometimes.

"Ankh," he said again. "An old Egyptian word. It has been interpreted many ways, but in this case, it means 'key to freedom.' It's where one goes to free oneself, from stress and other personal challenges. Your space ... your ankh."

He was so wise. Sara admired that about him. He knew so many things, so many different things. He was never at a loss for something to talk about. She was always happy in his company. He was not only easy on the eyes, he was interesting, intelligent and stimulating. She smiled as she thought Jenny would definitely make a joke about that, especially the stimulating part. She would keep those words to herself.

"Well, my wise-assed friend, if you are really lucky, I just might share my ankh with you. But I don't expect it will be your ankh, just mine. You'll have to just shut up and deal with it." Sara loved joking around with Steve. And? She was really liking that word "ankh." Her special word from her special friend about her special place. She sneaked another peek at Steve's face. Gosh, he was handsome. Feelings developed in parts of her body that had long-since died, as far as she was concerned. Butterflies in her stomach. Chills and delights in other parts of her anatomy. She almost felt guilty, but not quite. She was reveling in her world at this moment.

Suddenly, Jenny appeared in the doorway with a horrified look on her face and fluid dripping on the carpet.

"Oh my god, Mom. My water broke! Oh my god. It's not time yet! Mom!" Jenny collapsed on the floor.

Chapter Eight

Sara had been standing at the hospital nursery window a good fifteen minutes, staring through the glass, waiting on her grandson to move. She just wanted to see a glimpse of movement from the tiny powder-blue bundle lying in the bassinette in the corner of the room. She glanced over all the other babies, and it seemed most of them wiggled or moved a little bit now and then. Of course, maybe it was just wishful thinking on Sara's part. This nursery was for the preemies and all the babies were very small. A few more hours and they would be allowed in to see baby Samuel. She didn't think she could wait much longer.

Just then, Steve put a hand on her shoulder and whispered, "Kissing the glass won't get you any closer to your grandson. Why don't you have a seat with me here? Or we could go get a cup of coffee in the cafeteria."

"Oh, Steve, I am just so excited to hold him and smell him and be the best grandmother that I can possibly be to him. You understand, don't you?" Sara was dead serious. She wanted in that room and she wanted to hold her grandson.

Steve chuckled a bit as he took her hand. "Well, I do understand one thing for sure. You will most definitely be an amazing grandmother to that little boy. There is no doubt in my mind." At that, he brought her hand up to his lips and kissed it softly. "Why don't we check Jenny's room and see if she's back from recovery yet?"

"She had a tough delivery. I doubt she's back yet. Why don't you go check and I'll stay here, just in case?" said Sara. Steve started down the hall as Sara continued, "Just call me on my cell if she's there and I'll come on down." She smiled at Steve, although he'd already disappeared around the corner.

He really had been amazing through all of this. He had scooped Jenny up when she collapsed, loaded her up into his car, and brought them both to the hospital. There were no questions, just action. It was as if he belonged in the scenario. Sara didn't quite know what to make of him and all his attention. She was indeed enjoying it though.

Suddenly, a nurse appeared at the nursery door and said, "Mrs. Billings?"

"Yes?" said Sara, standing up.

"Just wanted to tell you we are bringing baby Samuel near the window if you'd like to get a better look," she announced.

"Oh thank you! I sure would. I'll be right here waiting! Thank you so much!" Sara was hardly able to contain her excitement as she almost tripped over a chair trying to get closer to the viewing window. They wheeled baby Samuel right beside the window. Sara could have touched his little face but for the glass separating them. He was sleeping soundly, his little lips making the slightest of sucking motions. He was beautiful. Tiny but perfect. He'd been born only 5 pounds 10 ounces, but everything was developed and intact. They had been blessed.

While she stood there admiring her grandson, she noticed that a man approached the window and appeared to be searching for a particular baby. Sara figured him to be in his early 40's. She also noted that he was quite handsome. A man like that would be hard not to notice. She wondered if he was there as a brand new dad or perhaps a young grandfather? She was just about to strike up a conversation when her cell phone rang. She answered and it was Steve, letting her know that Jenny was now in her room. "Great! I'll be right there," said Sara while collecting her things and hurrying down the hall.

"Hi, Mom," Jenny said in a weak voice, as Sara entered her room. "Have you seen him yet? Isn't he beautiful?"

"Well, hello there, little Mommy! And yes, I just saw him, just on the other side of the nursery room window. I can't wait to get my hands on that delicious little darling!" Sara noticed how exhausted Jenny appeared, how her eyes would close every few seconds as if she were fighting sleep. "Honey, you should just try to get some rest. You are going to need your strength very soon!"

"I know, Mom. I just want to see him once again before I go to sleep. The nurse said they will bring him to me, but just for a few minutes. I'm trying so hard to stay awake for that. Help me stay awake, Mom. Tell me about Samuel. Do you think he looks like me?"

Jenny's speech was slowing and her words were beginning to slur. Sara thought they'd better bring the baby soon or Jenny wouldn't be able to hold her eyes open.

"I will go and see if I can find out what's keeping them," offered Steve. Sara smiled. Steve to the rescue, once again. He sure did come in handy. She must remember to thank him properly later on. Of course, just exactly what a proper thank you would be, she hadn't figured out yet.

"I had a dream, Mom," whispered Jenny.

"Oh? Want to tell me about it?" Sara was intrigued. Jenny hardly ever mentioned her dreams.

"I dreamed about Dad. He was holding little Samuel. They were in the woods. It was really strange. I think Dad was taking my son somewhere. I don't know. I just know I don't want to have that dream anymore."

Jenny had a faraway look in her eyes. A sad, resigned gaze. Chills ran up Sara's spine. Her thoughts immediately returned to her nightmare about Mark taking the baby from his crib. Jenny's dream sounded all too familiar.

The mood in the room took an immediate upturn, however, as Steve returned with the nurse and little Samuel. Sara positioned the pillows so Jenny could sit up a bit more.

"He's been fed and changed and, as you can see, has fallen sound asleep," said the nurse. "However, I don't think it would hurt one bit if we wake him to have a little chat with his Mom!"

Jenny had decided to bottle feed Samuel from the beginning, much to the dismay of her mother. It was her decision, however, and Sara had decided to stay out of it. The nurse gently lifted the baby and placed him in his mother's waiting arms. Tears flowed down Jenny's face, with the emotion mixed with exhaustion taking over. Sara felt the love in the room and the tears also welled up in her eyes.

The nurse said she would return in fifteen minutes to get the baby. As she left, Steve said, "I'm going to get a cup of coffee and give you a few minutes alone. Can I bring either of you anything?"

"I would love a cup of coffee, Steve, thank you," said Sara.

"I'm just fine, thanks," said Jenny, in between her coos and kisses for Samuel.

Fifteen minutes went way too fast, as Steve returned with the coffee and the nurse returned to retrieve the baby.

"Just five more minutes, please? Just five? I'm not ready to say goodbye yet," pleaded Jenny.

"I'll tell you what. I'm due for my break now. I will give you fifteen more minutes and pick Samuel up on my way back. How's that sound?" offered the nurse with a big smile.

"That sounds perfect! Thank you so much!" Jenny and Sara both chimed in.

"By tomorrow, you should be able to keep Samuel in the room with you and feed him yourself. So you want to get all the rest you can before then," advised the nurse. "I'll be back in fifteen."

"Should I take a walk or something and give you girls some more time?" asked Steve.

"No!" retorted Sara quickly "Please stay! We'd both like you to stay. Right, Jenny?"

"Absolutely. After all, you were an important part of the delivery team," said Jenny. At this, Steve produced a big smile and settled into one of the chairs.

"I think he looks just like you, Jenny," said Sara. "He has your nose, for sure, and the shape of his mouth is the spitting-image of yours."

"He has darker hair than mine, and his eyes are much darker. But I see what you mean about his nose and mouth," said Jenny.

"Were you ever able to see a picture of the donor?" asked Sara. "Did he have dark hair and eyes?" Sara hadn't asked much about the donor, because every time she tried, Jenny changed the subject. She really knew nothing about him.

Jenny said nothing as she looked up at the person who had just entered the room. Her mouth fell open.

"Hi, Jenny," said a handsome man with black hair and piercing black eyes.

Sara recognized this man. He was the one looking through the nursery room glass a few minutes before. What was he doing here?

"Hi, Sam," said Jenny cautiously, holding her baby even closer as if to protect him from this intruder.

"When were you planning on telling me about the baby, Jenny? He is mine, isn't he? What's going on? Didn't you think I'd want to be a father? I hope you know that I have rights here," stated this stranger, quietly but firmly.

Sara's head began to spin. "Jenny, who is this man? I thought you used a sperm donor bank? What is going on?" Sara almost didn't want to know.

"Mom, this is Sam. He's the baby's father."

Chapter Nine

Sara and Jenny both arrived at the baby's door at the same time. "Mom, I got this. Go on back to bed," said Jenny. "It's his feeding time. I have everything ready in the kitchen. Just have to warm up the bottle."

"I'm already up. May as well give you a hand. Make yourself comfy in the rocking chair. I'll bring his bottle up," said Sara. She hadn't been able to sleep through one feeding since Samuel came home. Even the softest cry would awaken her. The excitement of a new baby in the house made sleep seem almost unimportant.

Sara warmed the bottle and took it up to Jenny. She paused at the door and gazed in on her beautiful daughter holding her own baby. Her heart swelled with pride and love. Jenny had been right all along: this baby was bringing them closer together and making the world right again. Samuel hungrily took the bottle for a minute or two, then fell asleep. Jenny gently adjusted the bottle in his mouth, just enough to induce the sucking motion, and before you knew it, Samuel was again enjoying his bottle. After another minute or two, he fell off to sleep again. The whole spectacle brought smiles to Sara and Jenny.

"He's multi-tasking," said Jenny. "At two weeks old, he's already a multi-tasker! Takes after you for sure, Grandma!"

Her mom had always been a busy woman, keeping everything in order and accomplishing several duties at once. Jenny was never like that, however. She was more like her father, laid-back, with a bit of a Type-B personality.

"Nothing wrong with that," said Sara. "The world is getting more competitive all the time. The term 'multi-tasking' never existed when I was young. At least I don't think it did. By the time Samuel grows up, there will be a whole new word for the business of life. Infinity-tasking or some such thing." Sara laughed at her own silliness.

"Infinity-tasking! I love it, Mom! Maybe I'll have him a little T-shirt made with 'Infinity-tasker' on it and he'll be the very first one! A pioneer of taskers. How's that for jumping the competition?" Jenny loved joking around with her mother. And now they had Samuel to carry on with their own special comedy routines. She liked that idea.

With little Samuel fed, changed and sound asleep, Jenny and Sara headed on back to bed. Jenny, exhausted but happy, had no problem falling back to sleep. Sara, on the other hand, lay awake for quite awhile with too many things running through her head. She thought about the errands she would need to run the next morning. She made a mental note to water the potted plants on the patio. They were drying out as she'd all but forgotten them since little Samuel came home. She thought about Steve. Ah, Steve! How warm and good she felt whenever he entered her thoughts. She hadn't seen him in a few days as he'd been away on a business trip. He had called and said he would be over tomorrow, and Sara was admittedly more than a little excited about his visit.

And then, as if to ruin her perfectly lovely transition to welcomed slumber, the haunting face of Samuel's father entered Sara's thoughts. She wondered what would happen with that situation. They hadn't heard from Sam since the day he'd shown up in the hospital claiming his paternal rights. Sara really didn't know the whole story, as Jenny hadn't spoken a word about Sam since they came home. Sara decided she wouldn't press Jenny about it, but would rather give her the time and space she needed. It was starting to drive her crazy though, so if Jenny didn't speak up soon, Sara was going to have to ask. Surely they hadn't heard the last from that man.

Right on schedule, Samuel announced the beginning of the new day with his wails of hunger, and while Jenny took care of his needs, Sara hurried to get showered and dressed, then downstairs to get some breakfast on the table. As usual, she was mentally multi-tasking as she headed down the stairs. Her thoughts were interrupted with the sound of the front door bell. She checked her watch as she headed to the door, thinking Steve was quite a bit earlier than was originally planned. Smiling as she thought he had missed her so much he couldn't wait until the afternoon, she threw open the door and said, "Hey, stranger! Long time no see!"

Her smile quickly faded as she realized she was staring right into the face of Sam, the baby's father. There was, in fact, a moment of silence as their eyes met, with Sam not quite finding his words and Sara dumbstruck. "Uh, hello Sam," Sara offered first.

"Good morning. I'm sorry to come by so early, but I wanted to catch Jenny before I go off to work. Is she here?" asked Sam. Sara thought he looked a little tired, but he was indeed dressed for work in a nicely tailored suit. Sara guessed he must be pretty successful in his work.

"I'll see if she's available. Come on in," said Sara, leading Sam into the kitchen. "Can I pour you a cup of coffee?"

"No, thank you. I only have a few minutes," Sam said, quite firmly.

"I'll check on Jenny, then." Sara started up the stairs as Jenny was coming down with the baby.

"Honey," Sara said in a low voice, "Sam is here to see you. He's in the kitchen. I don't know what he wants. Do you want me to take the baby?"

Jenny's face revealed her concern. "Yes, Mom, take Samuel. I need to talk to Sam alone please. I'll call you down when we're through."

"Okay," Sara said and took the baby back upstairs to the nursery.

"Hello, Sam" said Jenny. "I'm surprised to see you. I thought we talked about this. I don't need your help raising Samuel. You have your life." Jenny took a breath and then, "Why are you here anyway?"

"Jenny, please hear me out. I tried to stay away. I did. But every time I thought of you and the baby, all I wanted to do was be near you." Sam was sitting at the kitchen table, leaning toward Jenny, pleading with his eyes.

Jenny tried not to look at his eyes. He had the most amazing, deep dark eyes that forced her to look into her own soul. Yes, powerful eyes. She must not let him muddle her thoughts! Jenny turned away and proceeded to pour a cup of coffee.

"Jenny, aren't you even going to talk to me?"

"I'm listening to you, Sam. That's all I can handle for now. I'm listening," said Jenny.

"I want to be a father to Samuel, Jenny. Please at least allow me that. I won't ask for anything else for now. Just let me be near my son," pleaded Sam.

Jenny almost believed him. "Won't ask for anything else? I think you're already asking quite a lot, don't you? After all, you just showed up out of the blue. I hadn't heard one word from you after that last, big argument we had where you stormed out of my apartment. Not one word. And you want to know why I didn't tell you about the baby then? Well! I never got the chance, now did I?" Jenny was getting angrier with each word. "And now you want to be a father? Oh please. Samuel needs better than that."

"Things have changed, Jenny. I'm not like I used to be. Things are not like they used to be," he said.

"How the hell are they any different?" asked Jenny. "All I am seeing is a lot more of the same old, same old. You show up when you want to and you disappear without warning. No change there." Jenny didn't care how much she still loved him, or how much she wanted to jump in his arms, she was not backing down. She had a son to protect now. Sam didn't need them. He had his own life. She just needed to figure out how to convince him of that.

Sam looked at his watch and arose from the table. "I have to get to work. Can we continue this conversation soon? Can I take you to dinner, maybe tomorrow night? Please, Jenny. Just give me some time with you. I know I can make you understand how much I need you and Samuel."

"I don't know. I need to think. You'd better get on to work," Jenny said firmly. She showed Sam to the door, closed it behind him and sank into the chair in sobs.

"Jenny, what's wrong? What happened? Are you okay? What happened? Jenny?" Sara said.

"Where's Samuel?" sobbed Jenny.

"He's in his crib, honey. I laid him down when I heard you crying. Please, tell me what this is all about. Is this Sam a bad man? I need to know, Jenny. Please."

"No, Mom. He's not a bad man. He's a man I fell in love with last year. He's an older man. He's forty-two, Mom. I'm thirty-two. And he's little Samuel's father. And I still love him, Momma. Damn it! I still love him," said Jenny, shaking and gasping for breath between sobs.

"Honey! What's wrong with being in love with your son's father? And it's okay if he's older. You love him. That's all that matters!" comforted Sara. She was just so relieved that Jenny had finally told her about Sam. Maybe she could sleep nights now.

"Mom, you don't know everything." Jenny looked at her mom and quietly said, "Sam's married, Mom. He has a wife and two children."

Sara was speechless. She pulled Jenny to her and held her while she cried. Sara's tears didn't come though. Her thoughts were of Sam and how she would like to break his neck. That man was not going to ruin their lives if she had anything to do with it. "It's okay, baby. Things have a way of working out. It'll be okay."

After awhile, the doorbell rang once again. Jenny headed upstairs, fearing Sam had returned and not wanting to face him again just yet. Sara was ready to give him a piece of her mind, but instead, she opened the door to Steve, smiling from ear-to-ear, and holding the largest stuffed panda she'd ever seen. Sara laughed. Steve had been shopping for the baby, no doubt. He entered without waiting for an invitation, placed the panda on the chair, turned to Sara and softly leaned in for a kiss. Sara was trembling. "I missed you," he said, as he kissed her once more.

"Oh? Looks to me like you had some company," Sara joked as she looked toward the panda.

"Oh him? He doesn't count. He's not nearly as good a kisser as you," said Steve. And with that, they strolled into the kitchen for some coffee.

Jenny stood over Samuel's crib, watching him sleep so peacefully, and thinking about what her mother had told her. She wondered if things would ever really work themselves out.

Chapter Ten

The first face that appeared before Sara was that of Mrs. Goldberg. She lived down the street, just on the other side of Steve's house. Her features were distorted but it was definitely Mrs. Goldberg's head, hovering just above the baby carriage, and floating along at exactly the same pace that Sara was walking. "What do you want?" asked Sara. She could feel the spray from the old woman's mouth as she laughed. Her teeth were brown like that of a witch and spittle dripped from her lips. She didn't say a word, just laughed as she floated along. Sara tried increasing her pace and even swerved off the sidewalk in order to shake the apparition from her path. She checked the baby. He was asleep, and for that, Sara was grateful. Suddenly the laughter stopped. Sara looked up and Mrs. Goldberg was gone.

Sara continued to walk down the street. The houses were beginning to look unfamiliar to her. Some were quite run-down, with unkempt lawns and trash strewn about. This was not the street on which she lived. How did she get here? Sara turned and looked back in the direction from which she had come and nothing looked familiar. Where was she? She turned back around to continue her walk and standing on either side of the baby carriage were four women, all very old, and all staring at the baby. Sara quickly covered the carriage so the women could no longer see the baby and asked, "What can I do for you?" She didn't recognize any of the women. They all stared at her, and she found it quite unsettling that each woman smiled with rotten teeth and brown spittle seeping out of their mouths.

"You! You are that widow. We know who you are! You are that widow. You! You have a grandson. We know about him. He is a bastard child. He has no father. And you! You are bedding a man not even a year after your husband's death. You! Shame. Shame on you. Shame on your family." The old women spoke in unison, as if connected to each other, as if the four were actually one.

Sara was shaking as she said, "My family is none of your business. Now leave me alone. I have to get home. I know you're not real. I know this is a dream. I'm going home now. Leave me alone!"

"You'll never go home. You! You'll never find home again. You! We know who you are. You can never go home." The old women's voices had turned to

chants. As Sara turned the carriage around and hurried back in the other direction, they repeated the chants over and over again.

"You'll never go home. You! You'll never find home again ..."

"Honey, wake up!" said Steve as he gently shook Sara's arm. "Honey, you're having a bad dream. You're home. Everything's fine." Sara awoke, startled and shaken, collapsing into Steve's arms. "You're soaking wet, honey. And you were yelling, arguing with someone out loud. That must have been one hell of a dream."

Sara said nothing. She just clung to Steve, shaking and sobbing. She felt completely drained as if she'd been running all night. She could still see those old women. She could smell them. Why was she having dreams now? Everything had been fine and she hadn't had a nightmare in ages. Why now?

"Are you okay, honey? Can I get you something?" asked a concerned Steve, trying to find the right words.

Finally finding her voice, Sara said, "I'm okay. I just want to forget about it. Would you mind putting the coffee on while I shower?" She gave Steve a light kiss and left the bed.

Steve called after her, "Coffee coming right up. I'll rustle us up some breakfast too, while I'm at it. Just come on down when you're ready."

Jenny and the baby were visiting friends upstate so Sara and Steve had the house to themselves, at least until dinner when his daughter and her boyfriend would be there for a barbecue. Steve was concerned about Sara and thought it might not be the best time for a barbecue. He would ask her after breakfast, if she would talk to him about it. She never talked much about her dreams, but Steve knew she had them. He had talked to Jenny and knew a bit about her past issues. He headed on downstairs, resolving to approach the subject when the time was right.

Sara brushed her teeth savagely, as if she were the one with the brown spittle-laced mouth. She scrubbed her body in the shower, as if the odors of the old women were seeping out of every pore. She thought about the dream and about the women and what they had said to her. Was her subconscious sending her on a guilt trip because she'd found love? And who the hell cared whether little Samuel had a father or not? Besides, he did have a father! Okay, so Jenny was not married, but that was not something that would have ever bothered Sara. So why was she dreaming of such things? Her past bad dreams had all carried some kind of message, but not all of them turned out to mean anything substantial. Hopefully, this was one of those dreams. Yes! This was just a stupid, unsubstantial dream. She would not think of it again. At least that was her plan.

Sara got dressed and headed down to meet Steve. She paused at the top of the stairs and gazed lovingly into the nursery. She missed little Samuel so much. She could almost hear his gentle coos and smell his powdery deliciousness. He was her heart, as was his mommy. Sara was glad that Jenny was able to get away with the baby and visit her best friend. Jenny hadn't been out socially in some time and even though she was taking the baby, this was still an opportunity to have some fun with people her own age. Sara's eyes fixed upon the christening gown lying on the dresser and her heart swelled with love. The christening had been the previous morning, followed by a lovely reception on their patio. The weather had been perfect, and baby Samuel entertained everyone with his bubbly, happy demeanor. After the party, Jenny and the baby followed her best friends (Samuel's new godmother and godfather) upstate for the weekend.

"Breakfast is ready!" yelled Steve. "Come and get it!" As he turned around to put toast on the table, Sara surprised him.

"I'm right here, silly. You don't have to yell. I can still hear. At least I could hear until you started yelling. Now I'm not so sure," she teased, smiling from ear-to-ear and throwing her arms around Steve's waist. "I'm super hungry. I hope you cooked enough for both of us, because if you didn't, this is all mine!"

Laughing, Steve turned and gave Sara a quick kiss. Then he pointed to the table, which was laden with bountiful portions of eggs, bacon, toast, juice and coffee. "I guessed as much and cooked everything in the fridge. I'm just having coffee and toast myself. Gotta watch my girlish figure."

"Just means there's more for me. Let's eat!" said Sara. Steve enjoyed Sara's appetite. In fact, there wasn't much about Sara he didn't enjoy. He was smitten and he was quite sure she was aware of that fact. He didn't know how it happened. His was a happy life once again, and Sara was the reason. He was worried about her dreams, however. Why was she having bad dreams now? Would she ever confide in him about them? He wanted to help but was clueless as to how. She would need to talk to him so he could better understand. He desperately wanted to help if there was anything he could do.

"Honey?" Steve asked, as Sara finished up the last of her eggs. "I have an idea. Since we have the place to ourselves, why don't we postpone the barbecue for tonight and just enjoy one another. We could order pizza and watch movies. Just relax, ya know, with each other? What do you think?"

Sara looked at Steve and right away he knew he had been busted.

"You are worried about that dream I had, aren't you?" asked Sara.

"Honey, I just think you might want to take it easy. I was actually hoping we could talk. You know, about your dreams? You need to let me in, Sara. I want to help. Yes, I'm worried. When you woke up, it was like you'd actually been someplace else. It scared me. It had to have scared the hell out of you."

Steve looked at Sara then took her hand and brought it to his lips. She began crying. She started to pull away, wanting to run, as she always did. This time, however, Steve pulled her to him and held her as she trembled and sobbed.

"It's all been so horrifying for me, Steve. I don't understand why I dream like that. It always has something to do with Jenny or the baby, and it's always bad. Sometimes really bad."

Sara proceeded to tell Steve everything. He led her into the living room and they spent the rest of the morning on the couch as she described each and every dream to the fullest extent she could remember. When she was finished, she said, "There you have it. All of it. I haven't even told my therapist the things I've just told you. Now aren't you just a little bit wishing you hadn't asked?"

Steve held Sara tight, tears running down his own face, and said, "No baby. I'm glad you got it all out. I don't know how you've managed to keep this all bottled up inside for so long." Sara looked up at him and he ached for her. He wanted to protect her and make it all go away. In fact, he was determined to do so. He kissed her sweetly, tasting the tears and realizing that there was nothing he wouldn't do for Sara. "It's all going to be okay now, honey. We will face this together and we will get through it. I promise I'm with you. You always have me. I love you, baby. Don't ever doubt that, no matter what comes up in those dreams."

Sara and Steve spent the rest of the weekend together. A soothing, quiet peace had come over Sara after confiding in Steve. They enjoyed each other's company and reveled in their new love. They cooked, played, slept, made love, and made plans. Sara and Steve were both filled with a new and exhilarating hope for the future.

Monday morning came quickly and Steve went off to his job while Sara worked in the flower garden beside the front porch. She wanted to be there when Jenny and the baby arrived. She couldn't wait to see them. She wanted to hug her grandson and she had so many wonderful things to share with her daughter. She kept glancing down the road as she worked on the garden. At one point she looked up and noticed someone walking down the sidewalk toward her house. Her stomach turned as she recognized the person to be Steve's neighbor, Mrs. Goldberg, taking a morning stroll as she had many other times. Sara waved at Mrs. Goldberg as she walked by, while remembering the dream. Mrs. Goldberg promptly returned the greeting, along with a big smile. Nice white teeth! Sara felt a sense of relief while secretly laughing at herself for being momentarily frightened of the nice old woman.

Soon after, Jenny pulled into the driveway and Sara immediately took off her gardening gloves and ran over to the car to help. Samuel had a big smile for his grandmother and Sara couldn't get him out of his car seat fast enough. Another car stopped along the street and a man got out and walked up the driveway toward them.

"Who's that, Mom? Do you know?" asked Jenny.

"No. Never seen him before," said Sara. He was dressed in a rather cheap suit and Sara thought his hair could use a good wash.

The man walked up to the two women, looked at Jenny and said, "Are you Jenny Billings?"

"Yes, why?" asked Jenny.

The man then handed Jenny an envelope and stated firmly, "You have been served."

Chapter Eleven

"Mom, what is this?" asked Jenny, shaking as she gave the papers she had just been served to her mother. It looked like Samuel's father was suing her for custody.

Sara looked over the papers carefully and then confirmed Jenny's suspicions. "Looks like Sam wants shared custody, honey. I thought you and he had settled this and he wasn't going to be a part of Samuel's life."

Tears streaming down Jenny's face, she placed a sleeping Samuel in the playpen and sat down on the couch. "I don't know, Mom. I'm really confused. I told him I wouldn't share my son with his family. I told him I didn't need his help and Samuel didn't need his parenting, which would have been sporadic at best. It's been weeks. I don't know what's gotten into Sam, but I'm damned sure going to find out!"

"Well I think the first thing we should do is find a lawyer. I'm going to call my friend Becka," said Sara, reaching for her phone.

"Mom, Becka is a corporate lawyer. She can't help us," replied Jenny.

"I know that," retorted Sara. "But she'll know someone who can help us." Sara got Becka's voicemail and left an urgent message. Then she joined Jenny on the couch, took her hands into her own, and looked into her eyes for answers. "Honey, are you sure you don't want Sam to be a part of your son's life? Are you sure that's fair? I think we're in for an uphill battle here, so you need to be certain this is what you want."

Jenny squelched the urge to scream at her mother. She was so angry at Sam for invading their lives and her heart once again. He had agreed to cut everything off, at Jenny's insistence, and go back to his little family and perfect life. Jenny had cried all night, then got up the next morning, dried her tears, washed her face, and got on with her life without Sam. It was settled and that was that. Except it wasn't. Now Jenny had to deal with it, and she would deal with it sooner rather than later.

"Mom can you watch Samuel a little while? I have an errand to run. I just thought about it," said Jenny as she grabbed her purse and keys and headed toward the door.

"What? We're in the middle of a conversation. What's so important that you have to leave now? I want to finish talking about this," pleaded a puzzled Sara. Her words were wasted, however, as Jenny had already slammed the door and headed toward the garage. Sara could hear the tires squeal as her daughter's car sped down the street. Sara felt a shudder as she gazed over at the playpen and realized where Jenny was headed. "Oh no," mumbled Sara. "I have a feeling this is not going to end well."

The door opened and a girl of about ten looked up at Jenny with an innocence that caught her off-guard. She hadn't expected Sam's daughter to answer the door. She really hadn't thought it out at all.

Before she could find her words, the girl yelled, "Mom! Someone's here! My Mom will be right here. Are you the new decorator lady?" The little girl smiled up at her and Jenny could see Sam in her features. In fact, she also saw her son's eyes. It was almost enough to bring her to tears, but she fought to remain calm.

Sam's wife appeared at the door and did not have the same welcoming face her daughter had displayed. "What can I do for you? Are you here to see Sam?" Jenny nodded. From her cold stare and words, Jenny realized Sam's wife knew everything. "You may as well come in. He will be back in a few minutes. My name is Karen, in case you haven't already heard. Please, come in and have a seat."

Jenny followed the woman into the living room, feeling very much like she'd made a huge mistake. "I really shouldn't stay. Can you just tell Sam I was here? It's about the papers …"

Karen interrupted before Jenny had a chance to get a sentence out. "The papers. Yes I see them in your hand. I am somewhat surprised, however, to see you here. I figured we'd be hearing from your attorney instead."

Again at a loss for words, and not particularly wanting to discuss her son with Sam's wife, Jenny was silent, her mind racing as she tried to sort out her next move. Suddenly, Sam entered the room. She hadn't heard a car or a door. Had he been there all along?

"Hello, Jenny. I see you've met my wife." Sam poured himself a drink and sat down in a chair opposite the ladies. "I told Karen everything after you and I had our last conversation. She's not happy with me, of course, but she has forgiven me. She understands why I want to be part of my son's life."

Jenny finally found her courage, and her words. "I thought we settled all this. I don't want my son shuffled back and forth between two different parents and two very different worlds. You were not there for anything except the conception. Why are you doing this? Are you punishing me because I didn't want you back?" Jenny, determined to present a strong front, held back her tears.

Sam looked over at his wife to see her reaction to Jenny's words, and saw nothing on her face but resolve. He looked back at Jenny. "This is not about you and me, Jenny. You and I are over. This is about our son. I have parental rights and I want to exercise them. I hired an attorney and papers were filed to seek shared custody. I will admit I did this to get your attention. I would settle for having him with me every other weekend, some holidays and a few weeks out of the summer. I think that's more than fair, don't you?"

Jenny's head was spinning. If he had indeed wanted to get her attention, he certainly had! "Obviously, I don't know you at all. The joke's on me, huh? You wanted to get my attention? Well you sure picked a hell of a way to do it. What happened to just talking to me about this first?"

"We were way past talking, Jenny. The last time we met, you did all the talking. Don't you remember? I pleaded with you just to give me a reasonable amount of time with my son and you wouldn't even let me hold him when I was there! Jenny, I don't want to take Samuel from you. I want to be a father to my son and I want my son to know his father. Now if you are not open to any of this, perhaps you should go and we can settle it in court." Sam got up and walked out of the room. Karen excused herself politely and followed after him.

Jenny sat there alone, the flood of memories returning from the last time she and Sam were together. He was right. She hadn't been open to his suggestions for Samuel at all. All she could do at the time was feel the burning in her heart from loving a man she would never have. He had never intended to leave his family, but he was fine with continuing their affair. There was something different in his eyes, though, she remembered. There was a distance. He wasn't there for her! He was there for his son. He just didn't want to drive her away. Jenny realized that Sam would have kept up an affair with her just so he could be near his son, if he had to. She felt sick to her stomach.

Jenny gathered her things and left quickly through the front door. As she drove home, her entire affair with Sam passed through her mind. He had been the great love of her life. She had always known it. And now? He simply wanted to be a father. He belonged to Karen and his daughters. And he belonged to Samuel. Like it or not, Sam would be connected to her son for life. Jenny pulled up in the driveway, turned off the engine, and cried. She cried with every part of her being. She pounded the steering wheel and cried some more. And when she was all cried-out, she was drained of the energy or motivation to move past that moment in time.

Sara had heard her daughter's car pull up in the driveway and looked out the window to see her crying her heart out. She watched and waited, knowing Jenny needed to get whatever was inside of her out. She didn't know what had happened, but her instincts were to let things be ... for now. Sara waited until Jenny collapsed on the steering wheel, then went to the car and helped her into the house. Jenny headed straight for the stairs and Sara followed. Her daughter fell into bed and Sara covered her up and stroked her hair while she lay there like a lost child. Sara's heart ached for Jenny. Jenny's heart ached for Sam. But somehow, a peace fell over them both. Sara turned off the light and left the room.

It was time for Samuel's feeding. Sara went into the kitchen to warm up her grandson's food, then retrieved him from his nap, changed his diaper and sang him a little tune. Oh how she loved her little man! She realized he had another grandmother that would want to feed him and sing to him, and her heart ached. She didn't want to share, but it was not up to her.

With Samuel happily fed and enjoying the busy mobile in his playpen, Sara gave Steve a call on his cell. He had been unexpectedly sent to Chicago that afternoon. Sara remembered thinking he hadn't mentioned business in Chicago before. She needed him. She needed his arms around her, his strength. She would have to settle for his voice.

"Hello?" a woman's voice came across the phone ... a sultry, almost impatient voice. "Hello?" again. Sara was frozen silent. She looked at her phone to be sure of the number she had called. It was Steve's number. "Hello?" once again. Then click and silence.

Chapter Twelve

Sara pressed redial. She'd never been one to back down from a challenge and this bitch was no match for her. Sara was pissed.

"Hello," answered the same female voice, only sounding a bit more agitated.

"This is Sara," she said, mustering up as much strength in her voice as was possible. "May I speak with Steve, please?" Making a command rather than a request, Sara was quite satisfied with her stance thus far.

"Hi, Sara. He's in the shower. I'm Megan, his daughter. I haven't seen you for quite awhile. How are you?" The voice on the other end of the line morphed into sugary sweetness. Sara wondered how anyone could change gears so quickly without missing a beat.

"I'm doing well, and you?" Sara answered. Steve had gone to Chicago to see his daughter! How had she forgotten that Megan was in college there? Steve only talked about her all the time. Sara, feeling stupid, didn't wait for a reply, but continued, "I didn't connect Steve's trip with seeing you in Chicago. I thought he went out there on business. Is everything okay Megan?" Sara knew Steve wouldn't have left for Chicago in such a hurry if there hadn't been a good reason.

"I'm doing okay now, thanks Sara. Wow, it really is odd calling you Sara. I'm used to calling you Mrs. Billings. What happened was I called Dad, quite prematurely, when I thought I was being evicted from my apartment. Turned out, Dad talked with the property managers and I'm going to be fine through the rest of the school year. Dad to the rescue once again! Everything's okay now, thanks to him." Sara could hear the love for her father in Megan's voice. But was there something else? Sara had the feeling she was being snubbed, but in a most polite manner. Why hadn't Megan identified herself the first time she called? Sure, Sara hadn't spoken, but her name would have been plastered all over the face of Steve's cell phone. Sara decided she should proceed with caution with Miss Megan.

"Well that's good. I'm so glad you're okay. I need to go and tend to my grandson. Would you please let Steve know that I called?" asked Sara, determined to get off the phone quickly before the conversation turned snarky or worse.

"I sure will. Take care, Sara." And with that short dismissal, Megan promptly hung up. Although Sara was relieved that the mysterious woman had indeed been Steve's daughter, she still had an unsettling feeling in the pit of her stomach. She was not looking forward to the upcoming barbecue when all three girls would be coming over. Thank god Jenny would be there, for backup if nothing else.

That night, Sara was unable to reach a restful sleep. She tossed and turned and finally opted for a sleeping aid washed down with a glass of Chardonnay. After a little while she fell into a troubled sleep.

Three figures were standing over her bed. They appeared to be female, but their faces were blurred. Their hands, however, were crystal clear, and all six hands were gyrating in her face. Her sight was blinded by glare from the rings. On every hand. On every finger, in fact. Each ring held a single diamond and each seemed larger and more brilliant than the one before. The women were chanting something, but it was not in any language Sara had ever heard. The women never touched her but she could feel wind from their hands whipping in front of her face. Suddenly, an overwhelming desire came over her to have one of those rings. She reached out to the dancing hands, trying to claim a ring for her own. Her own hands seemed to move right through the women's hands and although she felt the breezes, she was unable to touch or retrieve a ring. A heavy sense of sadness overcame her and she began crying uncontrollably. Then the chanting sounded more distant with every second and the hands diminished to five, then four, then three, then two then one. Then the rings, the hands and the women were gone.

Sara awoke to the early morning sunlight and a couple of very noisy birds just outside her window. She felt eerily rested yet most definitely shaken by the perplexing nightmare she'd just experienced. What, if any, significance did the dream have for her? As with all the previous dreams, Sara knew there was no definitive answer to that question. All she knew was that she was sick and tired of the dreaming. She got up, showered and got dressed, and went to the kitchen to put on some coffee. Then she settled into her chair at the dining room table, opened her laptop, and began the search for a new therapist. She'd paid a fortune for the last shrink and where had that gotten her? Apparently, right back in the same condition. Sara was determined to do something about the nightmares, and becoming a drug addict or alcoholic or both was not a viable option. The only answer was to find another therapist.

As she was looking through the listings, Jenny came into the kitchen with the baby. "Good morning, Mom".

"Morning, honey. How are you doing this morning?" asked Sara.

"Better, thanks. I have to move on, right? Samuel is my concern now and all my decisions will be made with his best interests in mind," said Jenny. Sara noticed her swollen, sad eyes and it made her heart ache for her daughter.

"Honey, whenever you're ready to tell me what happened yesterday, I'm here for you," offered Sara.

"Long story short, Mom. I went to see Sam, met his wife and daughter, and came to the realization that Sam needs to be a father to Samuel. I don't think I can continue to stand in his way. I'm going to allow visitation: pretty liberal visitation. It's the right thing to do," said a reflective, resigned Jenny.

"I'm sorry it was rough for you, Jenny, but I'm glad you are settled with how you want to handle this. I think it will be for the best, especially for little Samuel," said Sara, empathizing with her daughter while secretly hoping it could all be that simple. Somehow, things never were as simple as they should be. "I do think you should hire an attorney. There's still the matter of the summons, and you want to protect your rights."

"Yeah, I think you're right, Mom. Did you hear from your friend, Becka? Does she know anyone?" asked Jenny.

"Yes, she called last night with a referral. His name and number are on the counter," said Sara, going back to her research on the laptop.

"Thanks, Mom," said Jenny. "I'll call after I finish with Samuel and get him settled down. What are you up to this morning?"

"Oh, truth is, I'm looking for a new therapist. I'm having unwelcome dreams again, just about every night. They're not nearly as horrific as they used to be, but bad enough. I'm just trying to find someone who can help me understand what's going on without doping me silly," said Sara half jokingly, until she looked up and saw the concern on Jenny's face. "Honey! Don't worry. It's nothing I can't handle, but it's enough to cause some sleeplessness. I'm all right, really. I just want to see if I can get some help, that's all."

Jenny, satisfied with her mother's explanation, finished feeding Samuel, then cleaned him up and put him in the playpen. She poured herself a cup of coffee and joined her mom at the table. Looking at the attorney's name, Jenny said, "This guy sounds familiar, Mom. Do we know him?"

"No, I don't think so. Becka said he comes highly recommended, and she would know. So give him a ring. Couldn't hurt," assured Sara.

Jenny called the attorney's office and set up an appointment for that afternoon. "Can you watch Samuel this afternoon, Mom?"

"Hmm, let me check my schedule," teased Sara. "Of course I can watch my grandson! Nothing I like better than spending time with my little man!" She smiled at Samuel as he chattered happily to his toys that surrounded him in the playpen.

Jenny went upstairs and Sara made a few phone calls. She finally settled on a therapist and made an appointment for the next week. That being done, she cleared the table and loaded the dishwasher. The doorbell rang a few minutes later and Sara opened the door to her handsome and smiling Steve.

Sara, grinning from ear-to-ear, said, "Come on in, you!" She gave Steve a kiss and teased him, "And the next time you have to go out of town, it might be nice if you told me it is to see your daughter."

"How about the next time I just take you with me?" Steve said, smiling down at her. She had no doubt that he loved her.

"Good answer!" said Sara. "How's Megan doing? Is she okay? She didn't sound very happy on the phone."

"I think she just needs a break. She's having trouble with her studies and her finances, but she'll be all right. All the girls will be home for break on Friday.

Are we all set for the barbecue this weekend?" asked Steve.

"Are *we* all set?" asked Sara, with exaggerated sarcasm in her voice. "I am all set, but we are not all set. There is no we. You didn't prepare a thing. Just setting the record straight!" Sara laughed. Steve hadn't done a thing toward the barbecue except to decide to have one.

"Well just tell me what to do, Your Royal Highness, and I'll be your bitch. Not a problem." Steve laughed as Sara chased him into the kitchen slapping him with her dish towel.

Jenny arrived at the lawyer's office that afternoon, fifteen minutes early, had a seat in the reception area, and proceeded to check email on her phone. A few minutes later, a man appeared in front of her and presented his hand, "Hello, I'm Matt. You must be Ms. Billings?"

Jenny looked up into the handsome face of Matthew Joiner and almost forgot what she was doing there. "Yes, please call me Jenny." She took his hand and stood up, catching a faint scent of his cologne. She was impressed and more than a bit charmed, but she wasn't going to let him know that. "Joiner? Your last name sounds so familiar. Have we met before?"

Matt smiled and responded, "No I think I would remember you. You might be thinking I'm familiar from the ads on TV. My family has numerous and varied businesses throughout the city."

"That's it, yes! I've seen your name on billboards and TV and such!" Why was she driveling on and on like a love-struck schoolgirl? And who did this gorgeous hunk of man think he was, that he could render her a stuttering mess with just a smile? She had to get control of herself, and quickly. Jenny cleared her throat and said, "Shall we get on with this? I have other appointments this afternoon."

Matt led Jenny to his office and motioned her in, "Please have a seat and tell me what I can do for you, Ms. Billings." Jenny's heart was racing and beads of sweat were forming on her forehead. What was going on? She hadn't been this 'bothered' since Sam. Jenny smiled as she realized she really was still alive and well.

Saturday arrived all too soon and Sara was busy preparing side-dishes and dessert for the barbecue. Jenny was marinating the steaks and preparing the vegetables to be grilled. Steve would have virtually nothing to do once he arrived except to actually operate the grill, which he had insisted was the most important job. Sara was a bit nervous with Steve's three daughters also coming and, except for the brief phone conversation with Megan, Sara hadn't had much contact with them over the past few years.

The doorbell rang and Jenny said, "I got it, Mom."

"Thanks, honey," said Sara, with her hands busy frosting the carrot cake she'd made. Steve had said carrot cake was a favorite of all the girls. She wasn't fond of carrot cake, and neither was Jenny, but this barbecue was all about the coming together of two families, and Sara wanted to please.

Steve and the girls came into the kitchen and said their hellos and gave hugs. Sara couldn't help noticing the resemblance of all the girls to their father. Megan and Maggie, the twins, were dark, tall, and beautiful, much like their father. Melissa, the youngest, had light brown hair and a lighter complexion than the twins. She seemed to favor her mother the most. All three girls had Steve's smile, wide and welcoming.

Steve headed out to the back yard to fire up the grill and the girls settled into the living room playing video games and fussing over little Samuel. Everything went beautifully. The food was perfection and the stories and fun flowed freely. After supper, Jenny and Steve's daughters dug in for a competitive volleyball game, while Steve, Sara, and Samuel watched from the picnic table. Occasionally, Steve would put his arm around Sara's waist and speak to her softly, words only for her. Sara felt happier than she had been in years.

Later, everyone helped with cleanup while Jenny took Samuel upstairs for his bath. The girls and Sara took everything into the kitchen and began cleaning and putting things away. Steve headed out to the store to pick up another bottle of wine, as he said he wanted to celebrate with her privately later. Sara was looking forward to that.

Just as she wiped the last spot on the counter and turned around to wipe the table, she met the cold stares of three young women with something on their minds. They stood in unison, all three lined up across the kitchen with their arms crossed and defiance on their faces. Sara braced herself for what was about to hit.

Megan spoke for the group. "We hope you are not thinking about marrying our Dad, because we are *not* okay with it."

Chapter Thirteen

"You want to know what I'm not okay with?" stated Jenny firmly as she brushed past the girls and stood with her mother. "I'm not okay with your coming into our house and disrespecting my mother. Trust me, you don't want to tangle with either one of us. We come from a long line of bitches."

"We're not trying to upset anyone," said Megan. Sara wondered if the other two girls even had tongues of their own, since Megan seemed to be the one who talked for them all the time. "We just thought you might want to know how we feel."

Sara had just about had her fill of their feelings but calmly said, "I have three responses for you. Take them and then please leave. One, marriage has not been discussed between your father and me; two, if marriage had been discussed, it would have been between the two of us and none of your business; and three, should you insist on making it your business, we would all have to sit down with your father and discuss it. I'm not sure you would want that."

"Why don't we just discuss it right now?" Steve's strong voice broke the uncomfortable silence in the room.

"Hi, honey," said Sara. "The girls were just giving me their opinion about our upcoming nuptials. Color me surprised but I don't think they are quite on-board with the union." Steve put his arm around Sara and glared at his daughters.

"Dad, we were just …" said Megan, but her father would have none of her excuses.

"I am so disappointed in the three of you at this moment, I can hardly think. The first thing I want you to do is apologize to Sara for this outburst, and then I want you to go home. Now!"

Sara hadn't seen Steve like this before. All this time, she'd been thinking he was spoiling the girls and they pretty much ran the show. Not now. She was impressed.

The girls all whined in unison, "We're sorry, Sara."

Feeble attempt at best, Sara thought, but she'd take it. For now.

Before anyone else could say a thing, Steve commanded, "Okay, girls, now it's time to go. I'll see you back at the house." The girls took no time getting out the door.

Steve turned to Sara and Jenny and said, "I don't even know how to begin to apologize for their actions."

"No need," said Sara. "You just did, with the way you handled the whole situation. I appreciate that, honey." Sara was relieved it was over, at least for tonight.

Jenny said her goodnights and went on upstairs. Steve held Sara and for a moment no one said a word.

After a bit, Steve said, "Baby, about tonight, I think I'd better go on home. I hope you understand?"

Sara looked up at Steve, "Yes, you should go. I'm almost sure the mood has passed anyway." She grinned as she said it, and Steve reciprocated with a smile and a quick peck on the forehead.

"Okay, I'm off. See you tomorrow." And with that, he was out the door. Sara poured herself a tall glass of Merlot and sat down on the living room couch. She went over the evening's events. What the hell just happened? And even more puzzling was, how could those three snooty little hellions ever come from Steve? Suddenly, everything didn't seem so romantic anymore, but rather complicated. She did not want complicated.

Steve stormed in the door, threw his keys on the dining room table, grabbed a beer from the fridge and headed straight for the den. "What the hell just happened back there?" Megan was on her phone, Maggie on the computer, and Melissa was watching TV. All three jumped when Steve entered the room. "I want some answers! You sure weren't raised to behave that way. What has gotten into you, and why are you directing it all towards Sara? You know I love her, don't you? You are going to have to accept that because that's the way it is." Not giving the girls an opportunity to respond, Steve continued, "I don't know that I've ever been so embarrassed, for you, and this family. I am appalled at your behavior. Well? What do you have to say for yourselves?" Steve slumped down in the chair and waited for a response.

Megan spoke for the group, as usual. "Dad, we didn't realize it was getting that serious. Are you really in love with her? She's way older than you, Dad. We thought she was just trying to get her hooks into you so we let her know how we felt about it. That's all. We were just trying to protect you." Megan saw Steve's face begin to turn red again, so she sat down and stopped talking.

"Protect me? From what? A kind, beautiful woman who makes me laugh and makes me happy? Wow, excuse me if I don't appear grateful, but I don't need or want your protection." Steve was growing angrier by the second and thought he'd better just end this conversation for the night and pick it back up once he'd calmed down and had some time to think.

"I'm going to bed. We'll discuss this tomorrow," he said as he left the room.

"We're really sorry, Dad. Goodnight, Dad ..." Megan called after Steve but he'd already headed upstairs. She looked at the other two girls and said, "Well we sure screwed this one up didn't we?"

Jenny came downstairs with the baby while Sara was pouring the coffee. "Morning, Mom. You doing okay?" asked Jenny.

"I'm fine, honey, just a little tired. I drank the rest of the wine and wallowed in self-pity last night. It was bound to catch up with me." Sara smiled as she made fun of herself. She deserved the hangover headache. She should have just gone on to bed instead of finishing off the bottle and crashing on the couch.

"Well I sure hope Steve lit into those brats when he got home. All the nerve!" said Jenny. Ah, her strong-willed Jenny. Sara loved her and her defiance.

"I'm quite sure Steve has everything under control. I was proud of him and the way he handled them last night. I'm sure those young ladies have had an earful by now." Sara could have thought of some more select, colorful words to describe the girls, but decided to be a grown-up about it, at least in front of her daughter and grandson.

"A good old-fashioned whooping is what they need," said Jenny. "Especially that Megan. What a smartass."

"Don't hold back, honey. Tell me what you think." Sara laughed, although she was thinking exactly the same thing.

Changing gears, Jenny remembered she had heard from her attorney. "Mom, I'll need you to watch Samuel tomorrow morning. My lawyer called and said we need to meet with Sam and his wife regarding the papers that were served. I think I may have done a lot of damage by showing up at their house unannounced. I'm worried about this meeting."

"Do you think Sam will continue with the suit for shared custody? I don't understand how he'd ever win shared custody. He didn't have anything to do with the baby until now," said Sara.

"I know, Mom, and I had decided to give him liberal visitation. However, now they want to meet with us. It doesn't sound good to me, Mom. I'm biting my nails," confessed Jenny.

"Well try not to worry until you actually have something to worry about. Maybe they just want to solidify some details. Wait and see. And of course I'll watch Samuel," said Sara.

Monday morning came all too soon and Jenny arrived a few minutes early to talk with Matt before the meeting. "Good morning, Jenny! You look wonderful!" said Matt, extending his hand.

"Looks can be deceiving because I'm sure not feeling wonderful. Do you have any idea what's going to happen in there?" asked Jenny, hoping for the best.

"Please sit down, Jenny. May I get you some coffee or a bottled water?" asked Matt.

"No I'm fine, thank you," Jenny replied, anxious to get on with things.

"Okay, well I can tell you that these types of meetings do not usually occur unless terms of the counter offer have been rejected. So my initial guess is that they desire something more than just visitation. We will soon know for sure, though," said Matt.

"He is not taking my baby, I can tell you that for sure," said Jenny.

"Please try to relax, Jenny. We will do everything we can to make sure that does not happen," assured Matt.

The door opened and in walked Sam, his wife, and their attorney. Everyone said their hellos and the meeting began.

Sam's lawyer spoke first, "We have gone over your offer of visitation and we are here to let you know we decline. We no longer feel that visitation is enough.

We are proceeding on with seeking shared custody of Samuel."

Jenny felt her face grow hot and her hands begin to tremble. Matt covered her hand with his and spoke before she had a chance. "We are not amenable to shared custody. Liberal visitation is quite generous and it is our final offer."

Sam and his wife sat there, remaining silent and quite calm, as if they'd done this a thousand times before. Jenny wanted to jump over the table and slap the serious right off their faces.

"Don't you have anything to say Sam?" Jenny spat out. Sam's lawyer motioned them not to respond. Jenny was not to be ignored. "What, can't speak for yourself? We're talking about a little baby here, Sam. A baby you know nothing about except that he carries your DNA. A baby who has only known his mother. A baby that does not deserve to be shuffled back and forth between houses and families every week, never really knowing where he actually belongs. This is not right, Sam, and you know it. Don't do this just to punish me. Please!"

"I know no such thing," said Sam, not willing to be silent any longer. "It would not be right for me to sit back and let you claim most of my son's life. I love him too."

"You just want to win. Winning is everything to you." Jenny couldn't stop herself.

Sam's lawyer finally took control of the meeting. "Excuse me, everyone. Thank you. We are obviously getting nowhere here. As we cannot come to an agreement, it would appear we will be settling this in court."

Matt looked at Jenny, trying to find some semblance of a fight in her. He didn't have to wait long.

"That's right, bring it on! Let's settle this in court." That being said, Jenny got up and left the room. Matt gathered his things and went running after her.

As he caught up with her, Matt said, "Wow, you were amazing back there! I think we have them admiring our brass balls if nothing else."

"Thanks, but I don't feel like much of a success right this minute," said Jenny.

"Things are going to work out, Jenny. Hang in there with me. I have yours and Samuel's best interests in mind and in my heart," offered Matt. He hugged Jenny, trying to squelch her fears. He wanted to help this woman so badly. Every time he was near her, he felt drawn to her, and this was all becoming quite personal for him.

Jenny, trembling in his arms, pulled away and managed a weak smile for him. Then, wiping tears,

Jenny got in her car and headed home. All the way home, she replayed the meeting in her mind over and over again. If Sam wanted a fight, then a fight was what Sam was going to get!

When Jenny arrived home she saw Steve's car in the driveway. She hoped it was just Steve and not his three spawn of the devil. She let herself in the door, put down her keys, purse and brief case, then strolled into the kitchen for a drink. As she entered the room, she saw little Samuel sitting happily in his carrier, amusing himself with oversized plastic beads. Then her eyes averted to the main attraction in the room. There at the kitchen table, sat her mother, looking down at a kneeling Steve, hand outstretched, and tears running down her face.

"Could you repeat that one more time? I don't think I heard all of it," cried Sara.

"My beloved Sara. I love you with all my heart. Will you make me the happiest man in the world and say you'll marry me?"

Chapter Fourteen

"How did that make you feel?" asked the therapist, leaning on folded hands and looking over his reading glasses. Sara was slightly amused that he looked like an actor trying to play a therapist. However, she'd been sitting there for an hour with him and her amusement was waning fast. At last count, she had been asked the same question five times.

"How do you think it makes me feel?" Sara replied. "I'm marrying this most wonderful man and his daughters are completely against us. And dreaming about them isn't helping my nerves much, I can tell you that." She had been having the same dreams with the three women standing over her bed, just about every night since she'd accepted Steve's proposal. Every time, they dangled diamond rings in front of her face and then disappeared. "A less evolved woman would surely take the dreams as a bad omen and run from the whole situation, don't you agree?"

"I do indeed agree, Sara. However, you are evolved. You know that dreams are just that, dreams. From everything I've heard here today, I am confident that those dreams are nothing to worry about. You have handled every obstacle in your life with determination and grace since your husband passed away. The dreams were an outlet of sorts. They have become less and less severe as your life has been repaired and rebuilt. I believe they will dissipate with time." The doctor sat back in his chair as if his job was done.

Sara asked, "So it's as simple as that? I don't need therapy, just time?" She leaned forward awaiting the important diagnosis.

"Yes," said the doctor, "as simple as that. Go out there and make your life what you want it to be, Sara. You have many memories to make." With that the therapist got up and offered his hand.

Sara took it and thanked him, gathered her things, and left. As she walked toward her car, she felt the warm breezes on her face and she felt lighter. Her thoughts drifted back to Steve and she smiled. "I'm getting married! Everything will work out. I will make sure of that." As she got in her car, she gave Jenny a call and said, "Hi, honey. Want to meet me for lunch?"

"Sure Mom. What's the occasion?" asked Jenny.

"Well, we're either celebrating my clean bill of mental health or the fact that I just spent $300 for absolutely nothing. Either way, I'm hungry." Sara laughed. She was feeling better by the minute.

That following Monday morning, the doorbell rang early. Sara opened the door to Matt, Jenny's lawyer. "Hi, Matt. Come on in. Jenny's getting ready and shouldn't be long. Want some coffee?" Matt followed her into the kitchen and had a seat at the table, where he took out his laptop and phone.

"That would be great, Sara, thanks. I need to check on a few notes while she's getting ready. We need to have all our ducks in a row for this hearing," said Matt.

"You bet you do!" said Sara. "My grandson is not going to live with that man! Is there anything I can do to help?"

"Actually, I think we have a good case. Just giving Jenny your support will be important. She needs to remain calm throughout this entire hearing. I can't stress that enough. The judge we're seeing has no patience whatsoever with emotion," offered Matt.

"I'll do what I can, Matt. Unfortunately, I raised a very emotional child. She calls it like she sees it," said Sara.

"Well, if we both remind her?" suggested Matt. He'd been getting to know Jenny and he knew she didn't take well to being bossed around. He liked her, a lot, so his approach would be gentle.

"Remind me of what?" asked Jenny, as she walked into the kitchen with Samuel on her hip. "What are you two up to? It can't be good. Come on, fess up!"

Sara decided to take the reins. "We were just talking about the judge and his intolerance for resistance. He needs to be handled carefully. Make sure to smile and be gentle with him, Jenny. I know you can have him wrapped around your little finger if you put your mind to it."

Jenny produced a big grin as she placed Samuel in his high chair. "His Honor will be putty in my hands. Not to worry." Sara could tell Jenny was putting up a brave front. She was nervous all right. Sara noticed her hands shaking a bit and a twitch in her eye. Jenny always got a twitch when she was nervous. Sara decided to let it go. Jenny needed to handle this on her own.

"Well, Samuel and I will be just fine and will be waiting for your phone call with the good news," said Sara.

"Mom, thanks for watching Samuel so much lately. You have a wedding to plan and I haven't been one bit of help with all this custody stuff going on," said Jenny.

"Oh the wedding's a couple months away, and it will be small, so we have plenty of time. I would like you to go with me to try on dresses, though. I think we should take care of that pretty soon," said Sara.

"I'm looking forward to that! You're not going to make me wear some fluffy chiffon or girlie lacey stuff, are you? I am not down with that, Mom," joked Jenny.

"But honey, I heard chiffon is making a comeback." Sara laughed, and then continued, "But not to worry. I'm really feeling something with more simple, tasteful lines, such as a straight shift-type dress in a subdued pastel. Blue perhaps. What do you think? You're my only attendant so I want you to love what you wear." Sara was trying to take Jenny's mind off the hearing, and it seemed to be working as her eye-twitch had disappeared.

"So you're really not going to ask Steve's girls to stand up with you, Mom?" asked Jenny.

"Well, I did give it some thought, for about five minutes. But no, I'm sure there will be enough drama without the thought of having to put those three in wedding attire. I don't even want to think about it." Sara laughed but really wasn't kidding. She was sure the girls would refuse to be attendants anyway. In fact, she hadn't seen them at all since the night of the barbecue. The twins had returned to college and Melissa was busy with her friends, according to Steve. They would all be in town again soon, though, so she was bracing herself for "round two" and hoping for the best.

Matt cut in, "Jenny, we'd better get going."

"Okay, just let me get my purse." Jenny went upstairs as Matt headed on out to the car. After retrieving her purse, Jenny popped back in the kitchen to say goodbye to her Mom and little Samuel.

"Give me a call as soon as you know anything, honey. I'll have my fingers and toes firmly crossed," said Sara as she gave Jenny a quick hug.

"Love you, Mom" Jenny kissed Samuel and then was out the door.

Sara poured herself a cup of coffee and sat down at the table with her grandson. "Well my little man, it's just you and me. What shall we do? Maybe we'll work in the yard for a bit. Yes, I think that's what we'll do." Sara stroked Samuel's hair as he crunched on his Cheerios, one by one with his four teeth. He was so precious. Sara's heart ached when she thought of their home being broken apart by the possibility of shared custody. It just couldn't happen. It was not the right thing for Samuel and she hoped the judge would see that.

Steve called a few minutes later from work. "Heard anything yet?"

"Oh god no, it will be hours yet, I'm sure," said Sara "I'll be a nervous wreck by that time, I'm also sure. How's your day going?"

"I have one meeting after another lined up, or I'd be right there with you. Sorry, honey. I'll check in with you later though. Love you!" replied Steve.

"Love you too, baby." Sara hung up the phone and finished up breakfast with Samuel. After cleanup, they went out to the back yard. Sara filled the kiddy pool for Samuel to play in while she worked in the flowerbed. Samuel loved the water and squealed with delight while splashing away. Sara kept a watchful eye on him while she trimmed weeds, enjoying the peacefulness of the beautiful morning and the joy of her grandson.

The huge double doors opened and everyone spilled out of the courtroom. Jenny could hardly contain herself and before reaching the hallway, she jumped into Matt's arms, exploding with happiness from the verdict just rendered. Jenny would have full custody of little Samuel and Sam would be allowed scheduled, unsupervised visitation to be determined through mediation between the parents and their attorneys. "We did it! Oh my god, we did it Matt! Thank you! Thank you so much!" squealed Jenny, not holding back one second longer. She'd held her tongue and upheld the decorum requested by her lawyer and her mother. Now it was time to celebrate!

Sam and Karen came out of the courtroom and brushed past Jenny and Matt without saying a word. They were not happy with the judge's decision. Jenny watched them disappear down the hall and then giggled, "Don't go away mad, Sam. Just go away!" Then she hugged Matt again and they made their way out of the courthouse. "Oh gosh, I've got to call Mom, now." Jenny dropped her things on the nearest bench, sat down and dialed her Mom.

"Hello? Tell me the good news. I'm waiting," said Sara, quite seriously.

"Full custody, Mom! We got full custody! He gets visitation, and that's fine with me. Oh gosh, Mom, I am so happy. Hug my baby for me, will ya? I'll be home soon," said Jenny, still hardly containing her excitement.

"I sure will, honey. I'm so happy for you! We will celebrate tonight. I'm thinking pizza and a couple of sappy old movies, just you and me and Samuel. Sound good?" offered Sara. She just wanted to share this night with her daughter. The guys, except Samuel of course, would have to find something else to do.

"Sounds perfect, Mom. Can't wait. I love you, Mom! See you in a bit." Jenny hung up the phone and they headed toward the car.

"Would you like to join me for dinner tonight to celebrate?" asked Matt.

"Oh Matt, I'd love to, but I have plans with my mom and the baby tonight. I hope you understand. Rain check?" Jenny hoped Matt wouldn't be upset. She really did want to get know him a lot better.

"Sure. Maybe next weekend? Dinner and a movie?" he wanted something secured before he let this go.

"Sounds good. I'd love to. We'll get Mom and Steve to babysit and have the evening to ourselves. How's that?" she asked. Jenny liked him and she wanted him to know it.

"Sounds wonderful. Looking forward to it already. Now let's get you home to that little man of yours!" said Matt with a satisfied smile on his face. Today had been a good day. He was proud of his accomplishments in this case, but more importantly, feeling very fortunate to have Jenny in his life.

The following Saturday morning, Sara and Jenny left Samuel with Jenny's friend and went to the bridal shop to try on dresses. Sara had no intention of wearing a full bridal gown, but she'd checked online and this particular shop had a nice selection of dresses to suit all tastes and ages. They checked in and were taken to a nice private section of the store where there were comfortable chairs and a coffee table laden with hors d'oeuvres, coffee, and champagne. The ladies had a seat and the sales staff began bringing samples of dresses for their perusal.

"Oh, Mom, I love this place! And forget the coffee, I'm having champagne. How about you?" asked a delighted Jenny.

"Definitely, the champagne." Sara giggled. "After all, I won't be doing this every day. In fact the next time will be when you are trying on wedding gowns!"

"Oh, I know the day you're talking about, Mom. That would be the day hell freezes over. I'm not ever wearing one of those heavy gowns. Not my style. I'm getting married in Vegas wearing a bikini, a big floppy hat and a smile," joked Jenny. She looked over at her mom and her heart swelled. Her mom looked so happy, she was glowing. This brought tears to her eyes that she quickly wiped and tried to hide.

"Are you really my daughter? And if you are my daughter, how did you get to be so stubborn?" asked Sara. Without waiting for an answer, she reached for the champagne bottle, turned it up and took a big swig. Jenny's eyes got as big as saucers. "What? I can be spontaneous too! Really I can. I might not ever wear a bikini to my wedding, but I do know how to have fun. See?" Sara joked as she took another swig.

"I love you, Mom," was all Jenny had to say. It was a perfect day.

That night Jenny and Samuel went for a sleepover at Jenny's friend's house. Sara and Steve fired up the grill, opened up a bottle of Merlot and enjoyed each other the way engaged couples do. They made love long into the night and when Sara finally fell off to sleep, there were no dreams, just peaceful rest.

Sunday morning came with a knock on the door. Steve was in the shower and Sara was making pancakes. She wiped her hands on her apron and went to open the door. She was expecting Steve's three girls to come over and join them for breakfast so she assumed it was them. She was not looking forward to the meeting, but knew it was one she had to meet head-on and deal with.

However, the girls were not at the door, but rather two uniformed police officers. Curiously, they just stood there, not saying a word.

Sara, swallowing a lump in her throat, managed, "Can I help you, officers?"

Chapter Fifteen

Sara's heart pounded as she waited for one of the officers to answer.

"Good morning, ma'am. We're looking for Steve Mathers and were told that he might be here. Have you seen him?" asked the officer on the right. The other officer stood stone-faced and motionless.

"Yes, he's here," said Sara, her heart still pounding away. "May I ask what this is regarding?"

"I'm sorry, ma'am, we need to talk with Mr. Mathers." Sara figured that was coming.

"Come on in. I'll go let him know you are here," said Sara. As the officers entered, Sara noticed the police car in the driveway, and a young woman in the back seat. She was almost positive it was Melissa. She closed the door, motioned the officers into the living room, and made a beeline for the stairs.

Steve was getting dressed when Sara walked into the bedroom. "Honey there's a problem downstairs. The police are here and it looks like Melissa is sitting out in their patrol car. I didn't get a good look, but I am sure it's her, and the police are not telling me anything. They want to speak with you."

Steve took Sara's hand and quickly headed down to the living room. "Hello, I'm Steve. What's going on? Is that my daughter in your patrol car?" Steve wasn't wasting any time with pleasantries. His blood pressure was rising rapidly.

"Yes sir, we have Melissa in custody. She was taken from a party where there was under-age drinking. We drove her to your house but no one was home. Melissa told us you might be here. She did nothing wrong other than be somewhere she shouldn't have been, so we are releasing her to you. No charges will be filed. Please talk to your daughter about this." The same officer spoke as before. The other remained silent.

"Thank you officers, I certainly will do just that. Can I see my daughter now?" said Steve. Sara breathed a huge sigh of relief that the situation was not as grave as it most surely could have been.

The officers led Steve out to the patrol car and turned Melissa over to him. Sara stayed behind in the living room, feeling Steve would want to take the reins at that point. Steve thanked the officers, took his daughter's arm and escorted her inside the house. No words were exchanged until they reached the living room, when Steve simply said, "Sit down." Melissa obeyed.

"Would you like me to give you some privacy?" asked Sara.

"No," Steve replied quickly. "Please stay honey." Sara sat down on the couch next to Steve, facing Melissa.

"Dad," began Melissa, "please let me explain." Melissa's eye makeup was smeared down her face from the tears. Sara handed her a tissue.

"I'm listening," said Steve in a calm but stern voice.

"I went to the party with Megan and Maggie. I was just tagging along. We were only supposed to stay a few minutes and then go out to eat. It was a huge party. I got separated from them and the next thing I knew the police arrived," offered Melissa. Sara thought she was believable but there had to be more to the story.

Without so much as a flinch, Steve asked, "Where are your sisters?"

"Dad, I don't know. I haven't seen or heard from them since. And I lost my phone. I couldn't call anybody. I'm so sorry, Dad." Melissa was crying again. Sara could tell that she hated disappointing her father.

A short knock on the door, and in walked the twins, followed by Jenny and the baby. "Oh my God, there you are!" said Megan to her little sister. "We have been looking for you all night!"

"Sit down," Steve commanded to the twins. Jenny gave her mother a questioning look and then walked through the living room and on up the stairs. She decided it was not something in which she needed or wanted to participate.

The twins and Melissa began to quarrel and voices became louder and heated. Sara was getting quite uncomfortable and could not understand why Steve was just sitting there. Finally, when she'd had enough, she spoke up. It was her house after all. "Girls! That's enough! This is getting us nowhere. One at a time, please." Steve gave her an approving glance, as if he was relieved she was helping. Sara thought that maybe Steve just didn't know what to say.

"What business is this of yours?" Megan said, shooting daggers at Sara with her eyes.

That woke Steve up. "Wait just a damned minute, young lady! Do not talk to Sara that way. She is my fiancé and will soon be a part of this family. You will show her some respect!" Steve left no doubt in anyone's mind that Sara belonged beside him and had a voice.

Steve continued, "I'm not sure what went down last night, but everyone's safe and no one's in jail, so I guess that's a good thing. However, I take issue with you girls taking Melissa to such a party. And even more issue with your leaving her stranded. Now Megan and Maggie, you are grown women and what you do in your spare time is your business; but when you put your sister in possible danger, it becomes my business and we have a problem."

This time, much to Sara's surprise, Maggie spoke up. "You're right, Dad. We should not have taken Melissa to that party. I'm so sorry." Megan gave her a dirty look.

"It was a harmless party and we had friends there. How were we supposed to know there would be under-age drinking?" countered Megan.

"The fact still remains that you abandoned Melissa. This is unacceptable behavior. At the very least, you should have stayed right with her," said Steve.

"I know, Dad. And you're right. We're really sorry." It was Megan again, speaking for the group.

"Honey, I think they see what they did wrong. We've all made mistakes. Can we decide to just try and make better choices next time?" Sara said, attempting to begin closure, as she was convinced the girls had just had quite a scare and were remorseful for their actions.

"Yes I think we're done here," Steve said. He was clearly not happy with his daughters, but knew Sara was right. The issue had to be closed. Without another word, Steve went out to the backyard to check on the bird feeders. He just wanted out of that room.

"Thanks, Sara, for sticking up for us," said Megan. The other girls nodded in agreement.

"I think you see what you did wrong and have learned from it," replied Sara.

"But Dad's still really mad." said Melissa.

"Yes, he is. And he probably will be for a while. Just leave him alone for a bit. He'll come around when he's ready," said Sara. She knew Steve well enough. He needed his space right now.

"Ok, we sure will. Thanks, Sara," said Melissa. The girls got up to leave and Sara escorted them to the door.

As they left, Maggie turned around and said, "Sara, let us know what we can do to help with the wedding. We want to help." The other girls agreed.

Sara was surprised, as well as delighted. She hadn't seen that coming. "Thank you, girls. I will have jobs for all of you I'm sure! I'll let you know. And? We'll take a rain check on those pancakes," said Sara, figuring the girls needed sleep more than breakfast, and Steve just needed to be away from them for a while.

Sara closed the door, feeling things were certainly looking better on the home front.

Jenny came downstairs and said, "Is the coast clear?" She had put the baby down for a nap.

Sara put her arm around her daughter and said, "For now! Want some pancakes?"

"That sounds really good, Mom. So, I guess we're not watching our calories today? You do remember that we both have to squeeze into fancy dresses in just a few weeks, don't you?" teased Jenny.

"The thought never leaves my mind. And guess what? Steve's girls asked if they could help with the wedding. Can you believe it? Will wonders never cease!" said Sara.

"Wow, did Steve dive into them? Did they have a 'come to Jesus' moment? Do tell, Mom. I can't believe they'd offer without either a threat or a bribe? Fess up. Which was it?" joked Jenny, only she wasn't really joking.

"I think it may have been a combination of it all. The cops, Steve's disappointment, and then my support. Whatever it was, I'm grateful. They were on my list of wedding worries. I think I can strike them off now. I think," said Sara. She wasn't stupid, though. She would be watching them like a hawk.

"Well Mom, that is great! I am so happy things are coming together," said Jenny.

"Enough about the Mathers girls," said Sara "What's going on with you and Matt? And have you heard anything from Samuel's father lately?"

"Funny you should ask," smiled Jenny, "Because I have a dinner and movie date with Matt next weekend and was going to ask you to babysit."

"Of course I'll watch Samuel," Sara broke in right away, "and I'm very happy to hear you're finally giving that young man a break. He has been quite attentive and I think he's smitten with you."

"Yeah, yeah, yeah, Mom," replied Jenny. "We'll see about that. I am just going to take it slowly. Anyway, I wasn't finished. I said I was going to ask you, but turned out, Sam and Karen will be taking Samuel for his first visitation next weekend. In fact, Sam called and they seem very excited about it," said Jenny.

"Well they've certainly changed their tone. Glad to hear it," said Sara.

"It's not like they had much choice, thank God," said Jenny. "It was either visitation or nothing. I think it's going to work out. I was over at their house and I believe Samuel will be well looked-after and happy over there during his visits. I feel good about it."

"That's a relief!" exclaimed Sara.

"It sure is," agreed Jenny.

The next Friday evening, Sam and Karen showed up at the door at promptly 6 p.m. to retrieve little Samuel. Jenny had Samuel all ready and waiting for their arrival. She welcomed them into the living room where everyone could take a few minutes to acclimate to the situation. Sam and Karen were grinning from ear to ear and Samuel seemed to love the attention. Jenny watched them all together and for the first time, felt at peace with the arrangement. This was all going to work out. And Samuel deserved to know his father. Karen was okay, Jenny had to admit. "But," she thought, "if they didn't have Samuel back promptly at 6 pm Sunday evening, she'd have the cops on speed dial."

After Sam and Karen loaded up the car with everything the baby would need, they said their goodbyes, gathered up Samuel and started out the door. Jenny was watching from the door. Before they backed down the driveway, Sam got out and walked up to Jenny. "Just wanted to thank you for everything. We'll take good care of Samuel. Don't worry. I can't believe how much I love him already. Thank you Jenny." Jenny didn't say a word, but just smiled as Sam got back in the car and drove away. Then she headed upstairs to get ready for her first date with Matt.

The wedding day had finally arrived. The chapel had been decorated. The back yard had been transformed into a tented reception area and the caterers had their orders.

Steve and Sara slept in their respective homes the night before the wedding, holding on to the old tradition of separating the bride and groom.

Six o'clock a.m. at the Mathers house came and all was quiet. Everyone was still asleep.

Six o'clock a.m. at the Billings house, on the other hand, came and with it, a frenzied flurry of activity that didn't slow down the entire morning. The tables and chairs in the tent had blown over from a brief storm that had rolled through overnight. The rain had blown into the tent and there were puddles of water all along one side. Jenny and Sara were busy mopping and straightening up. After that, Jenny showered while Sara fed Samuel. Then Sara showered while Jenny settled Samuel in his playpen with his toys. He was climbing out of the playpen nowadays so Jenny had to keep a constant eye on him.

After some coffee and a little breakfast, the ladies did some quick dusting and vacuuming and touch-up in the bathrooms. They were expecting only about thirty guests for the reception, but thirty people could fill up a house really fast. They couldn't afford to have extra clutter, so moved everything that wasn't necessary out to the garage. By that time, it was 9 a.m. and Steve was nowhere in sight. He was supposed to take the ladies to pick up their dresses and the flowers. They needed to be back before noon to accept delivery of the wedding cake and greet the caterers. Everything had been scheduled down to the wire and there was not much room for deviation.

At 9:15 a.m. Sara gave Steve a call. Sure enough, he had overslept. "I'll be there in ten minutes, I promise," he said. Sara was timing him. He showed up in exactly ten minutes, and to Sara's surprise, had all three girls with him.

As they entered, Steve exclaimed, "I made it! And I brought reinforcements. The girls are here to help. Just tell them what you need."

Sara couldn't mask her big smile. This was an answer to her prayers. "Good morning ladies! So glad you're here. We actually do need someone to watch Samuel while we go pick up dresses and flowers. Would you mind watching him?"

Megan spoke up, "I think the three of us can handle that cute little man, yes!" She walked over to the playpen and picked Samuel up, and he immediately broke into squeals of laughter. Sara smiled thinking what a flirt he was turning out to be.

"And," added Steve, "you can pitch in and clean or cook or whatever needs doing."

The girls all nodded and set about their duties. Sara looked on, thinking this day might just go smoothly after all. She'd just be happy if nothing major went wrong. It was a huge help to have the girls on her side now.

It was 2 p.m., just two hours before the wedding. A big storm cloud ascended on their house, and produced a hard downpour for about ten minutes. As soon as the sun came back out, everyone was in the back yard mopping, drying, cleaning and reorganizing. After just a few minutes, the reception area looked perfect again and everyone went to get dressed for the ceremony.

Jenny appeared in the doorway of Sara's room in her Maid of Honor dress, and Sara held back the tears of happiness as she gazed at her beautiful daughter. "You take my breath away, Jenny. I wish I had the words for the love I feel for you. I hope you know."

Jenny hugged her mother and said, "I know, Mom. Me too." They finally broke their embrace and Jenny produced a small box with a bow. "Mom, you know the something old, new, borrowed, and blue tradition? Well, here's your something old."

Sara opened the box and picked up a delicate lace handkerchief, perfectly pressed, with faded signs of age and the letter "M" embroidered in the corner. She recognized it immediately as her own mother's handkerchief. It had been left to Jenny when she died. It was one of Jenny's most precious possessions.

"Thank you honey," said Sara, choking back the tears once again. "This is perfect, just perfect."

"Can we join the party?" interrupted Melissa. She and the twins were standing at the door, all carrying little boxes with bows.

"Sure, come on in!" exclaimed Sara. "It may take the four of you to get me in that dress. Are you up for a challenge?"

"Ready and reporting for duty!" joked Megan. "But first, we have something for you. Melissa, you go first."

Melissa presented Sara with the little box and said, "Here is your something new."

Sara opened the box to find a tube of her favorite lipstick. "How did you know?" she asked. She didn't need an answer, though, when she saw the big smile on Jenny's face. "Never mind. I see you all have been conspiring!"

Maggie stepped forward and presented her gift, "And here is your something borrowed. It was my mother's. I hope you will wear it. I think it will go beautifully with your dress."

Sara opened the box to find a stunning single diamond pendant necklace. "I would be honored, Maggie. Thank you so very much." The tears were getting tougher to hold back.

Finally, Megan presented her gift, saying, "Hmm, what is missing? I think it might be your something blue!"

Sara opened her last gift to find a sexy, lacy blue garter. "Well this should liven things up considerably! Thank you Megan. Thank all of you girls. I have no words. I'm just so happy."

"Well then, let's get you ready to face your groom!" said Jenny.

The double doors to the chapel opened. The guests were seated. The groom, the best man and the pastor took their places up front. The double doors closed. A few minutes of anticipation, and then the double doors opened once again. The bride, on the arm of her daughter, took tiny steps in time with the music. Their movement was slow and calculated because Sara wanted the moment to last. She wanted to savor every second, see everyone's faces, and feel all the emotion welling up inside her.

On her right, Sara saw her old friends from work and her best friend who was holding little Samuel. She paused just long enough to give him a kiss, much to his giggling delight. She saw Steve's girls on her left, all so beautiful and looking every bit like their handsome father. She smiled through her happy tears and each girl returned her smile. Were those tears in Megan's eyes? She saw Matt on her right and gave him a wink. The next wedding would be Jenny and Matt's, she was quite sure.

Sara and Jenny reached the end of the aisle. Jenny relinquished her mother's arm to Steve. They faced each other and held hands.

Sara lifted her head up, locked her gaze on her handsome Steve, and thought, "Somebody pinch me. I surely must be dreaming again!"

Acknowledgments

I would like to thank my partner, Joan Timmerman, and my sons, Abe Oros and Glenn Sonoda, and daughter-in-law, Amanda Oros, who have supported me in the writing of this book, as in every other challenge I have faced. A special thanks goes out to my dearest friend, Mary Barker, who has never stopped believing in me over our thirty-plus years of friendship. Mary also provided the beautiful sketch of Sara's house featured in this book. Thanks also go out to Karla Telega, and the folks at Adoro Books, for their support and guidance. They also created the beautiful cover art for Sara's Sleep. My loyal readers, Vidya Sury, Rachel Speer, Brenda Bowman, Tracy Wilson, Janet Mitchell, Donna Brown, and my sister, Robin Craig, also deserve a grateful nod. Their support and encouragement were invaluable to me.

About the Author

Mom, Grandmother, full-time Grad student and professional job-seeker Terri Sonoda has added writing to her repertoire with the release of her first novella, *Sara's Sleep.* Terri lives in Las Vegas, which explains her passions for video poker, SPF 64+ sunscreen, big sunglasses, and watered-down tequila. She is an avid reader, computer nerd, and chaser of dreams. She enjoys writing fiction to include humor, romance, and drama. You can delve into her diverse observations and talents on her blog at www.terrisonoda.net.

Made in the USA
Charleston, SC
13 June 2012